T0315964

A Jewel for a Jacobite

Bronwen Hughes

Onion Custard Publishing Ltd

A JEWEL FOR A JACOBITE
BRONWEN HUGHES

First published in Great Britain 1980 by Robert Hale Limited.

Revised and reprinted by Onion Custard Publishing Ltd.

www.onioncustard.com

facebook.com/onioncustardpublishing,

Twitter @onioncustard

First Edition, ISBN 0-7091-8283-X, 1980, hardback.

Second Edition, ISBN 978-1-909129-573, 2014, paperback.

ABOUT THE AUTHOR

Born and bred in Cardiff, South Wales, Bronwen started her career in The City Library during the 1940s. Since then, her writing career has spanned six decades. She has written over 400 short stories for magazines, and has had several novels and poems published under the names *Bronwen Hughes* and *Bronwen Vizard*.

All of Bronwen's earlier work was produced on a typewriter with several layers of carbon paper, while the production and re-printing of this book has utilised modern digital technology.

A Jewel for a Jacobite is set in her native Wales. Having moved away from the area for a while, Bronwen returned to South Wales in the 1960s and still lives there surrounded by family, including six children, sixteen grandchildren, and an ever-increasing number of great-grandchildren.

BRONWEN

PROLOGUE

At first Catrin thought that the man was dead. He lay on the stone floor of the ruined building, his arms spreadeagled and protruding from the inadequate cover of a cloak which carelessly tumbled over his still body. Curling, blond hair clung in wet tendrils to the waxen flesh of his temples and cheek. His head, in clear-cut profile rested immobile on a cushion of rushes and Catrin felt the same chill which had brushed her when she had once visited the Cathedral at Llandaff and had stood beside the carved effigy on an ancient tomb.

The man's face appeared to be hewn from the same stone, but Bess, who had been the first to push through the ever-greens which shrouded the entrance to the shelter, nosed forward and roughly licked the man's hand. Catrin bent down to push the dog away but as she did so the man moved, in jerky, convulsive movements, and she saw that there was a hot, inflamed patch on each cheek and that tiny beads of sweat glistened on his forehead.

She held out her hand tentatively, and touched his brow. His skin was clammy, yet at the same time like fire. Although the cold December air struck a damp chill on the girl's cheeks, the man burned with his own raging fever. As he moved, the cloak slipped from his shoulders and Catrin could see the fine linen of his shift, linen more refined than any her father or brothers had ever possessed, but now soaked with sweat and clinging in tiny pleats to the contours of his frame. One sleeve was torn to the elbow and a bandage was wound roughly over the forearm; a bandage now stained with pus and blood and barely covering the swollen arm which throbbed with hidden fire.

The man lay near the door, as if straining to reach shelter, he had collapsed before he had fully examined his surroundings. His open pack spilled its contents, a cravat edged with exquisite lace, a small hide-bound volume, a leathern flask, rye bread, a hunk of cheese, over the beaten earth floor. The first rays of dawn crept through the open door and were reflected and magnified as they were caught by the chased silver hilt of a sword and the intricate and jewelled design of its scabbard. A mud-spattered tricorne hat and a coat of rich cloth, trimmed with frogged braid and with one sleeve patchily mended and stained with blood, lay in an abandoned and forlorn heap near the man's head.

His breathing was rapid and uneven and wove an unhappy harmony of sound with that of running water. Although at present shadowed and invisible in the darkness which still shrouded the opposite wall of the building, a stream ran, Catrin knew, along a narrow channel in the floor, from the spring in the hillside around which the structure was built.

She picked up the cravat, the delicate weave foreign and refined between her fingers, and bent over the gurgle of water. She smoothed the cool, wet linen across the man's forehead and he moaned slightly at such unexpected comfort. She moistened his hands, wiping away dust and grime, and gently bathed his neck where glistening rivulets of sweat crawled uncomfortably.

Catrin shuddered as she unwound the stained linen which swathed his forearm. The wound, which was open, was suppurating and the flesh around it flared with angry heat. Once again Catrin soaked the cravat and cleaned away the dark blood and yellow pus. Around her waist, she had tied to her girdle a cloth containing her breakfast. She felt thankful as she undid the knot that she had taken the trouble to collect the morsel from the farm kitchen before her ride to the hilltop. The bread and cheese tumbled from its wrapping and Catrin placed the food near the man's pack. He might be glad of it when he recovered, although at the moment the thought of eating would be far from his mind. Then Catrin wound the coarse linen cloth she had used as a wrapping for her provisions around the man's arm. She had no medicaments to apply. No soothing drink of camomile or borage which might reduce his fever. No charms or amulets which could call on supernatural powers for help. But the chuckling of the water in the narrow channel reminded her that the well was reputed to be holy. In the old days, people had travelled for many miles to this place on pilgrimage, occasionally someone still came, just to do what she had done for the unknown stranger.

He stirred. His eyes opened and Catrin gazed into clear, uncomprehending lakes of blue.

"You are fine," she assured him, in English because only an Englishman could afford such fine linen. "I will look after you. Bring you medicine."

She knelt near him, one arm circling Bess the rough coated collie, her fingers nervously tousling the dog's ears. She could see her breath, and the dog's, hanging wispily on the chill air of daybreak. The man's eyes focused. For a second he recognised another human form with relief, then even Catrin's ingenuous features, her curving lips and the dark compassion of her eyes, failed to avert the alarm which overcame him. He raised himself on the elbow of his good arm and tried in vain to gesture with the other.

"I must go… escape… run…"

He sank, exhausted with effort, and bit his lip as if the few words he had spoken were a mistake.

Catrin pulled the cloak across his shoulders and dragged the abandoned coat across to provide a more comfortable pillow for the man's head.

"You can go nowhere. You must rest. Don't worry," she added. "I am not going to tell anyone you are here."

The blue eyes gazed as Catrin's soft voice brought a measure of safety into the bleak building. He wanted to rest, to sink into oblivion, to lose mind and memory in a merciful haven of forgetfulness, and as Catrin's hand held his with gentle pressure, he gave himself over, abandoning himself to her care.

"This place… where am I?"

"Ffynnon Fair… St. Mary's Well," Catrin translated. "I will look after you." Then, as his eyes closed in sleep, added bleakly, "It is Christmas Day…"

ONE

The moon, swinging high over the valley, was circled with a watery rim, and spiky leaves of holly, black now that night had drained colour from the landscape, glistened with drops of the rain which had fallen most of the night. The farmhouse and its outbuildings straggled near an outcrop of rock, as if the protective hillside and the overhanging bushes might offer some shelter from the elements. Tonight, the stone roof reflected the moonlight on its wet surface, and the windows, shut tight against drips and draughts, stared blankly across the fields which sloped down to the river.

When the door of the farm kitchen opened, light spilled out on to pools of water which had collected in the ruts of the farmyard. A band of colour splashed across the bushes leaning over the gate, as if an artist, tired of the monochrome of midnight, had daubed leaf with deep green, and berry with brilliant red. Holly red, for the farmhouse, Ty Celyn, was named for the holly grove which on this part of the hillside momentarily ousted the luxuriant oaks and graceful ash trees which lined the beautiful valley of the Rhondda River.

Mrs. Thomas, for the moment protected by her pattens, which raised her feet above the soft red earth, waited by the door for Twm, the waggoner, to bring her horse. She held her hand out tentatively. To her satisfaction, it remained dry.

"Thank God, the rain has stopped," she muttered, and then as the man appeared leading two mares, one grey and docile, the other a chestnut of some spirit, she leaned back towards the kitchen.

"Hurry, Catrin," she called. "And be sure to bring the candles."

"I'm coming, Mother." Catrin appeared in the doorway, her cheeks flushed from the haste of preparation, her cloak fastened securely around her shoulders to keep off the chill of the night air. Behind her, three maid-servants stood in their outdoor clothes. "Jencyn has decided not to come," the girl added.

Her mother's lips tightened disapprovingly. "It was a mistake, hiring that man," she complained and then, noticing the look of dismay on her daughter's face added, "I'm not blaming you, Catrin. If only my stomach hadn't played me up, I'd have been at the hiring fair myself. You just haven't had the experience."

As the two women mounted their horses, Dic the shepherd brought ponies and mules into the farmyard for the rest of the household. Jenette and Mari and Jane giggled and jostled for places, Jenette determined to ride pillion behind Dic, because, as she had told the others in secret, at Halloween' her apple peel had fallen in the shape of a "D", and since then they had had an understanding. Finally they were all settled, and led by Twm, who rode with a lantern a little way ahead of Anne Thomas and her daughter, they trailed along the track which wove an uneven way between the fields bordering the river.

6

The two women guided their mounts in silence, Catrin uneasily aware that only a few months ago her mother would have been determinedly throwing around orders and commands, fussing about the maids' behaviour, arguing with Twm, demanding attention and obedience. Now, the very softness of her tones, her missing arrogance, her readiness to excuse when displeased reminded Catrin forcibly that this Christmas was very different from any she had previously known; that the year now dying, the Year of the Lord, 1715, had brought incalculable grief and tragedy into their lives. As they neared the ford across the swollen, grey river, Catrin wished she could turn her horse and gallop away, anywhere, south along the river bank to Cymmer, or high over Cefn Penrhys, or north to Blaenrhondda. She wanted to escape, to go any place except across the turbulent water of the Rhondda Fawr to the tiny church which stood on the opposite bank, and where the remains of her father and two brothers lay, shrouded by the dark flange of yew. Time had not yet repaired the disturbed turf in the churchyard, or the rend in the hearts of Catrin and her mother, and whenever she approached the ancient stone building the girl was poignantly reminded of their loss.

Tonight, as they neared the churchyard, noisy with assembling farmers and their households, bright with swinging lanterns, gay with ribald laughter and snatches of carol, Catrin felt desolation shroud her. The last time they had attended the Christmas *Plygain* service, her father had led their small band across the ford, closely followed by his sons, Will and Evan. Now, one short year later, only Catrin and her mother were left to run the farm, to discipline the servants, to celebrate the festivals which held the year in secure order.

Catrin glanced at her mother's face. At first immobile, mask-like in its rigid lines, as Anne Thomas neared the gathering, she smiled, fixedly and determinedly as if to dare anyone to challenge her delight of the occasion.

Catrin bit her lip. She doubted if she would be able to emulate her mother and pretend enjoyment, or even to see the service through without letting emotion overcome her.

In the vestry, Morgan Howell, curate of the parish of Llanfodwg, robed himself in readiness for the service. Already it was past four o'clock, the time he had hoped to commence, but the night had been wild and wet and many of his parishioners had to travel many miles, down hillsides and along valleys to reach the small church. He often blamed distance for the apathy amongst his congregation, but tonight he was assured of a good attendance. No one, except perhaps the sick or the very old, went to bed on Christmas night. The hours up to the service were spent in preparing the traditional dishes of Christmas Day, in setting up the Yule log, in decorating the houses with greenery, in revelry.

The service itself was a mixture of Morning Prayer and carol singing, many of the verses almost impromptu and written by aspiring bards for the occasion, and lasted until dawn, when Communion was celebrated.

"Shall I get them in, Vicar?"

Rhys, Mr. Howell's servant, a grey haired man

with a bent back and a limp, entered the vestry.

Morgan Howell winced at the title which Rhys insisted, which many of his parishioners insisted, on giving him. Each time he was addressed as Vicar, he was reminded of his lowly position as curate of a chapelry of Llantrisant, a position from which he seemed unable to rise.

"Are there plenty of people then, Rhys?"

Mr. Howell's bagwig was awry on his head, and he shivered slightly. The rush-light on the wall wavered in the draught, but here in the vestry it was reasonably warm. In the church itself the wind whistled through gaping holes in the roof and the curate postponed his appearance as long as possible. He had little fat about him and felt the cold.

"Middling, Vicar. Middling. Shoni is here with his harp and there are a couple of fiddlers as well."

Morgan Howell moved into the chancel as Rhys went into the churchyard to usher in the congregation who were busy exchanging news with neighbours seldom seen. The nave was dark, except for an inadequate rush-light on the wall by the door, but Shoni had taken up residence near the lectern and had placed a candle in a niche once occupied by a stone saint. As the congregation entered they lit their candles from the rush-light and either held them aloft, or perched them on ledges or on the remains of ornaments. The stone seats around the walls were soon occupied as were the rough benches in the body of the church.

Mrs. Thomas and Catrin, as freeholders, made their way to a bench near the chancel, but no one dared to sit on the seat on the opposite side. Morgan

Howell looked towards it as he picked up his Welsh copy of the Book of Common Prayer. Griffith Evans and his family would surely have arrived by now, had they intended to come to the service.

The murmur of voices died away and the jostling of bodies halted as the curate cleared his throat and Rhys gesticulated and urged order. The body of the church was now a blaze of flickering lights, which illuminated the cold faces of the worshippers, and threw a cast of gold over the rough homespun of their garments. In contrast, the recesses in the walls were thrown into deeper shadow, dark pools of mystery held at bay by the spell of the bright flames. The wretched timber of the arched roof, the crumbling stonework of the walls, the cracked paving, the trickle of water which spread over the floor of the chancel, were transformed by heavenly make believe.

"Mi a godaf, ac a af at fy nhad ..."

Morgan Howell spoke the words of St Luke in a deep, sonorous monotone which belied his spare frame. He paused. Outside, in the churchyard, a commotion arose. Sounds of horses neighing, a man cursing loudly, someone else giving orders in no uncertain terms. People's heads turned as someone banged on the door which Rhys had bolted lest the wind should tear it open.

He hurried towards it now. "Patience, Mr. Evans, Patience!"

He drew back the heavy bolt and Griffith Evans marched into the church. His sister followed meekly, holding the arm of a puny looking boy of twelve. His servants squeezed into places at the back while their master and his family made their way to the seat in the front of the nave.

Morgan Howell looked at the newcomer with barely concealed distaste, but felt obliged to bow as the man took up his place and looked about him. He hardly acknowledged the curate's greeting but inclined towards Mrs. Thomas and her daughter.

Anne Thomas jogged her daughter's arm and Catrin dutifully bobbed at Mr. Evans, but she looked down at the stone floor as she did so, averting her gaze from the speculative glance he threw at her from heavy lidded eyes.

As he slung his woollen cloak from his shoulders, his full-bottomed wig hung heavily over his richly decorated brocade coat. His face was florid, and he looked challengingly at Morgan Howell.

"You can begin now, Vicar," he said in English.

The curate understood the provocation behind the remark. He grasped the Welsh prayer book more closely and his gaze roamed over the congregation. Illiterate for the most part, and mostly monoglot Welsh, there were a few who had attended the school at Llantrisant sponsored by the Society of Christian Knowledge, and who had been taught to read and write English. Others, but very few of them, like the Thomases who could afford private lessons for their children, were more truly bilingual, but the vast majority of the people crammed into the church had no learning. They needed none to work in the fields, and spoke only the language which had been handed down to them by their forebears.

"We are all waiting, Vicar." Griffith Evans' lips curled and the wind chose that moment to send a flurry of rain through the roof and spatter the pages of the curate's prayer book.

He sighed as he placed it on the ledge beneath the lectern and substituted the English version. He had no option.

"I will arise and go to my father...." He began the service again, this time in English, and Griffith Evans patted his son's shoulder paternally and admonished him to take good heed.

Catrin was indifferent to the language the curate used. The words of the Prayer Book washed over her uncomprehendingly as she waited fearfully for the carols to begin. Fearfully, and at the same time with longing. Evan, the brother who had been one year her junior, had loved Christmas. Each year he had brought in armfuls of greenery from the hillside. Mistletoe to hang over the lintels, bright berried holly to splash the dark rafters with colour, ivy to trail around the hearth. Last year, he and Will had brought back the Yule log together and with much laughter had managed to kindle it with the help of some coal from the outcrop.

"Don't ever go to College," she begged Evan then, for later that year he was to have gone to Oxford, a place inconceivably far away.

"Don't worry, Catrin," he had assured her. "It will only be for a few years. Then when I am a lawyer, I will be able to put the family fortunes in order. And indeed, you are worrying too soon, for as you well know, I have another half year at Cowbridge first, and then a few months at home before I leave."

Catrin had not been comforted. A chill of prescience swept over her and she clutched her brother's hand possessively. "When you go, I think you will go for ever."

"Nonsense." Will their older brother had come into the farm kitchen and Evan turned towards him for support.

"Catrin is being dismal, and at Christmas time too."

"Then we must cheer her up." Will, tall and broad-shouldered and farm-minded like their father who was busy in the stables, had swung her round, and then raised his voice, singing some merry Christmas verses. Evan joined in as did the maid-servant who was busy at the *crochan* and a farmhand who had called in for a draught of beer. Soon the farm kitchen was alive with tapping feet and clapping hands, and Catrin's cheeks were flushed and her fears forgotten.

Now, in the damp church, close with the warmth of the tightly packed congregation, Catrin heard the harpist strike the same melody. First one voice, then another picked out a verse, then the crumbling rafters echoed with the chorus carolled out by the whole assembly. That scene, a year past, crowded Catrin's memory, with its poignancy, its premonition.

Evan had come back from his half year in school at Cowbridge in good spirits, but already marked victim to a particularly virulent strain of smallpox. On the day he was buried, Will and their father sickened and followed him on the melancholy trail to the churchyard. Life went on, but for Catrin it could never be the same.

She bit her lip and her cheeks felt moist as unbearable emotions swept through her. Anne Thomas, only too aware of her daughter's vulnerability, turned towards her anxiously.

13

"I must go," Catrin whispered. "I can't bear it. I shall only break down if I stay."

"Shall I come too?"

Catrin shook her head vigorously. "I must be alone, mother. Please!"

Anne Thomas nodded. She understood only too well how her daughter felt. She had no fears for the girl's safety. Even if the moon had not been lighting the way, Catrin's horse would find the trail, and footpads were rare in the valley. The inhabitants had little enough to steal.

Catrin pushed her way to the porch, scarcely noticed as the congregation sang lustily through the never-ending verses of the carol. Rhys looked at her in surprise but asked no questions when she asked him to unbolt the door. She stepped outside into the cold night air, and some of the tension slipped from her as she stroked Sheba's chestnut muzzle. Burying her face in the horse's long mane, she wept for the brothers and the father who had been taken from her so cruelly. The tears eased her a little and she sprang to the horse's back and turned towards the ford. The mare picked her way across it with accomplished ease. Catrin pulled on the rein when they reached the opposite bank. She had no wish to return to the farm. She wanted to ride across the hills, her hair loose in the wind, in the hope that memories and regrets could be flung away and blown to the horizon.

Her green habit constricted her, the tricorne hat, pressed firmly on her dark curls, prevented her escape from reality. She decided to spur Sheba towards the farm. She would change into something looser and wilder, and then travel the hill-tops until dawn brought the churchgoers back to breakfast.

She tethered Sheba near the door and was surprised to see a light flickering in the farm kitchen. When she entered she saw Jencyn ap Dafydd sitting near the hearth, a rush-light burning slowly on the arm of his chair, a large Bible on his lap.

For a moment Catrin felt a spark of unreasonable annoyance. The chair had been her father's special one. When a child, hers had been the task of trimming the light which was fixed to one of the arms and making sure that his pipes were nearby for him to relax when he had finished the toil of the day. Now she felt Jencyn to be a usurper, taking over something which did not belong to him.

"You are back soon, Mistress Catrin."

"And I see that you have not bothered to go to your bed."

"I am reading the word of the Lord."

"You could have heard it spoken if you had attended the church."

"In my own language, Mistress Catrin?"

Catrin flushed. "You know that Mr. Howell normally holds his services in Welsh."

"Should I then place myself at the mercy of Mr. Griffith Evans, as the Vicar does?"

Catrin turned on her heel and went upstairs to her room. She carefully placed the good green cloth riding habit in her chest and with relief put on a simple gown of homespun with a white linen fichu at her throat. She shook her hair free over her shoulders and pulled the hood of her cloak up to protect her from the night air. As she crept back downstairs she hoped that

Jencyn might by some good fortune have left the kitchen. She was unlucky and he threw a sharp glance at her when she re-entered.

"You are going out again, Mistress Catrin?"

"That's right." The man's deference grated, and was, she felt, somewhat false. "If my mother returns before me, you might tell her that I will be back for breakfast."

Catrin, in spite of her despondency, was a healthy young woman, and the very word "breakfast" brought a pang of hunger. Ignoring Jencyn, she lit a candle and went into the buttery to cut herself a hunk of cheese. She found some bread and folded both morsels of food in a linen napkin which she fastened through the girdle at her waist.

Bess, the collie dog who had been sleeping near the hearth, shook herself drowsily as Catrin unlatched the kitchen door.

"Good dog, Bess. Come on then. We'll have a run."

Catrin did not look back at Jencyn as she left the house and rode away on Sheba, the dog scampering ahead like a scout, excited by the raw night air and the unexpected outing. For a few miles, Catrin followed the track which stayed near the course of the river, unseen now beneath shrouding mist, but audible as it tumbled over rocks and swirled in frantic eddies on its way to its confluence with its sister, the Rhondda Fach.

"Bess, to heel, Bess." Catrin whistled and recalled the dog as she wheeled Sheba away from the river. "We're going to the top, old girl. Right to the top of Cefn Penrhys."

Only the wild air on the cap of moorland at the top of the mountain could cure her despondency. Only the dawn touching the close cropped turf with pink fingers, bringing life to the gaunt, leafless branches of the valley oaks, could brush away her tears.

In a damp, stone building, high on the hillside, Lord Simon Nichol lay in a feverish stupor. Once he opened his eyes and, through a wide gap in the roof, saw in the sky a cloud obliterate a star. Mostly he was unaware of his surroundings, oblivious to the cold and the discomfort. Jumbled images raced through his brain, mocking time and space, bringing back distorted memories, caricatures of experiences and events.

Sometimes he was back at the court of St. Germaine, playing courtier to a forlorn monarch, ignoring the patches of poverty, the insecurity of a life of charades. Sometimes he was a child on his father's estate in Derbyshire, chasing a rabbit with old Rob or following the hunt as it raced across the wild moorland. Sometimes he heard the crack of gunfire, the whine of shot, the agonising calls of dying and wounded. Sometimes he was aware of his arm burning like fire, the sweat which poured from his body, the fever which was likely to finish him and so end the nightmare chase and the fear of the hangman's noose.

Suddenly he was aware that he was not alone. Cool water flowed over his brow, his arm was dressed and became easier, somehow or other his head lay more comfortably on the rushes piled on the earth floor.

He opened his eyes and as they focused, his

understanding returned. A dark haired girl was bending over him. Momentarily he thought he was gazing at the statue of the Madonna in the chapel at St. Germaine, but although this girl had the same raven hair and milky complexion, her face was fuller and more vital. Her lips parted nervously as she spoke. Simon could not understand all she said, for she seemed to be speaking from another world, but he knew that she was reassuring him. The alarm which had sprung within him, urging him to flight was soothed.

"I will look after you," he heard her say, and the words echoed in his brain, lulling him, beckoning him to safety.

"I will look after you..." and then, unbelievably, as his eyes closed and he gave himself over to merciful sleep, "It is Christmas Day."

TWO

When Catrin left, Jencyn ap Dafydd closed the heavy book on his lap and extinguished the rush-light on the arm of the chair. The glowing Yule log now provided the only source of illumination in the kitchen, but its red glow was sufficient for Jencyn to find his way to the door which led to his sleeping quarters. Originally a simple, long farmhouse, Ty Celyn had been enlarged and extended at one time and another until it could almost claim the status of manor house. But in spite of numerous outbuildings and stables, in winter, the best of the dairy cattle were still housed in the stalls which formed an integral part of the old dwelling.

The loft above provided comfortable enough bedding for some of the unmarried farmhands, and the heat rising from the beasts beneath rendered it reasonably warm even in the coldest weather. Jencyn could find his way up the narrow ladder and to his section of the loft without light, and placing his precious book beside his other volume, *Bardd Cwsg,* The Sleeping Bard, a lurid description of death and hell, he plumped up the hay to make a satisfactory resting place. He was not tired even though dawn was not far away. His slight frame was wiry and this time of the year did not provide enough back-breaking work to drive away the restless images which prevented sleep.

He hadn't realised before coming to Ty Celyn that he was an ambitious man. The twenty five years of his life which had been spent in a Carmarthenshire village had been hungry years of poverty, only relieved by his conversion. A revelation which had brought faith, and if not hope, then acceptance into his life. A dissident minister had taught him to read in Welsh so that the Bible was his constant companion, and had also insisted that he acquired the skills of reading and writing in English.

"Jencyn," he had admonished. "You are a hard-working man. God will give you opportunities. You will want to take advantage of them."

So Jencyn had studied hard during the hours that his fellows were busy dancing, and singing and revelling; all occupations that Jencyn had objured when he had accepted the stern, dissenting faith.

His skills had impressed Catrin when she had attended the hiring fair at Llantrisant some months previously. Her mother was ill with the cramping pains in the stomach which had become so frequent of late, and Catrin was somewhat overwhelmed by the responsibility put on her. Her great fear was that she might hire some waster who would spend his time drinking and idling the hours away. This would have been disastrous for the farm now that it was deprived of the dedication of her father and elder brother. So when Jencyn presented himself in his drab but tidy coat, and spoke of his sober ways, and proved his ability to read the notices pinned to the walls of the Town Hall, Catrin hired him with relief.

Her mother had not been so sure of her wisdom. "We want a ploughman not a bailiff," she had exclaimed despairingly. "What good is reading and writing for a man who has to sow, and reap and flail and weave cloth in the winter?"

But Jencyn had proved a good worker too, although as the weeks passed Catrin began to share her mother's doubts. The evenings in the farmhouse, which had once been so merry, were subdued enough without her father's deep throated laugh and Will's jokes, but now whenever someone told a bawdy story, or Griff the clog-dancer turned up to entertain them, Jencyn would sit in solemn disapproval in a dark corner. Even Shoni the harpist failed to please, except when he put aside his ballads of love and intrigue and sang only of the wisdom or wrath of God.

But as he sat in his shadowed alcove, deep stirrings of ambition would rise inside Jencyn. Frustrating stirrings because he could see no way in which they could be fulfilled. He wanted to be master of a farm such as Ty Celyn. His occupation as farmhand employed only a fraction of his ability. All around him he could see evidence of mismanagement. Twm was easygoing and the other hands took advantage of him. The threshing could be done in half the time and release men to work in the loom shed. At present only enough cloth was woven to provide the household with its needs, but why stop there? Extra cloth would fetch a good price in the market. Jencyn could even think of methods of increasing the cows' yield, and so to make more cheese which could also be sold.

There seemed no way in which Jencyn would ever attain his dream, but inside, illogically, the certainty grew that one day he would achieve his end.

His faith in God, his conviction that his renunciation of pleasure would be rewarded, his prayers, sustained him. "Ask and you shall receive," it had been written. Jencyn asked that he would one day be master of a farm like Ty Celyn.

The clatter of horses hooves in the farmyard and the noisy chatter of the returning churchgoers roused him from the light sleep which had overtaken him, and he stumbled down the loft ladder and into the kitchen. The grey light of dawn now subdued the glow from the hearth, but the great iron *crochan,* the pot slung above it, steamed and filled the room with the aroma of mutton broth.

Anne Thomas entered, closely followed by Jenette and the other two maids.

"Fetch the platters, Jenette, and Mari, the oatcakes are on the dresser. Serve everyone straight away. I am going upstairs for a few moments."

Her face was drawn. Unusually, she looked considerably older than her thirty eight years. Her riding habit hung loosely about her. She had lost a great deal of weight since her husband's death.

"Mistress Thomas." Jencyn stood between her and the inner door. "Your daughter has gone out on Sheba. She asked me to tell you that she would be back for breakfast."

"Thank you, Jencyn."

Anne Thomas spoke irritably. The man's words were civil enough but he still annoyed her. Pushing him aside, she was too dispirited to give him more thought as she left the room and climbed the stairs to her bedroom. She wished she could cry, but her tears

22

had been spent months ago, leaving her desolate on a bleak plateau. As she changed into her workaday clothes, a twinge of pain in her side caused her to pause momentarily and to rest on the edge of the big bedstead.

The room was full of memories. It held the ghosts of lost hopes and dreams. She and Harry had lain beneath the quilted cover of the wide bed and had made plans for their sons and for the future of the farm. Anne had been proud. Anxious to rise in status. The family had suffered for generations, first from their recusancy, for they had clung desperately to the old faith for many years, then from their Royalist allegiance. The Thomases had always been on the losing side, like so many of the stubborn people of the *Blaenau* -the Hill People. Even at the Restoration, although now ostensibly in favour, they did not receive back any of the fines which had been extorted from them in the days of the Protectorate. Those days were long since past. German George sat uneasily on a throne many said did not belong to him, but Anne was determined that for once the family would go with the tide, whichever it was.

When Evan showed sign of ability she had urged Harry, her husband, to educate the boy at Cowbridge. This meant taking out a further mortgage on the farm, a debt which he accepted unwillingly.

"Evan has brains," she had urged. "He will make a lawyer. The money we spend on him will return ten-fold."

She had had visions of the success of the farm, of their acceptance by the country families, of a position of authority for Harry. He might even make Sherriff one day, although watching him help the stable-boys muck out the stable, or sink into his chair, tired and mud-stained at the end of the day, she had to admit that it was unlikely.

Now the dreams had dissolved into a nebulous wisp of bitterly remembered longings. The farm was in greater debt than it had ever known, and to Griffith Evans who had shown little mercy to other farmers in similar circumstances. She remembered Harry's reluctance to take out the mortgage with Evans.

"He will not hesitate to foreclose if we can't meet the debt," he warned her. "He has grown fat on the misfortunes of the hill-farmers."

Anne had been determined to have her way. She recalled her attitude now with dismay and sinking fear.

"We've got to do this, Harry," she had urged. "For Evan's sake. And for the farm too. When he is a lawyer, Evan will put the place on its feet."

"Not by double-dealing and twisting the law's precepts," Harry retorted angrily. "'I would rather Ty Celyn were razed to the ground, than we should gain fortune that way."

But he had given in, perhaps because he too wanted to see Evan take advantage of the education only money could buy.

Anne bent double for a moment, the pain which swept through her momentarily distracting her mind from tormenting regrets.

The spasm died and she straightened and remembered the invitation Griffith Evans had proffered after the service.

"Enjoy my hospitality at the New Year," he suggested. "You Mrs. Thomas, and of course, your daughter."

She thought about the invitation as she made her way back to the kitchen and tried not to feel revulsion at the way the man's eyes had swept over her, as indeed he had eyed Catrin at the beginning of the service. A calculating appraisal with more than a hint of sensuality, as if he were weighing assets and judging their value. Griffith Evans' second wife had died about a year ago, and Anne Thomas realised with a pang that she was an eligible widow, still quite young and with quite a slice of property.

As she entered the kitchen, Catrin came in through the outer door, and a flurry of cold wind sent the smoke from the Yule log eddying in dusty whirls over the heads of the merrymakers, who were still enjoying their Christmas breakfast.

Catrin found a platter and helped herself to a good portion of the steaming broth. The raw morning air and the excitement of her adventure on the hillside had brought a warm flush to her cheeks and a sparkle to her eyes.

"You enjoyed your ride, Mistress Catrin?"

Jencyn handed her the plate of oatcakes, deferentially yet, Catrin thought, with a certain inquisitiveness.

"Very much."

She smiled, but her lips were stubborn. Her imagination was persuading her that Jencyn was probing. Suddenly she felt that her secret was blazoned over her. That everyone must know she had been high on Cefn Penrhys, tending someone who somehow or other had fallen foul of the law. In confusion she threaded a way across to her mother, escaping from Jencyn's piercing black eyes, his suspicious words.

She sat on a bench and supped her broth silently, watching the activities in the farm kitchen as if they were some sort of charade. Two of the maids were exchanging secrets near the hearth, but Jenette had inveigled Dic to a place under an overhanging bunch of mistletoe and was drawing his attention to it with sly looks and coy blushes. He stole a kiss and then another, and growing bold slipped his arm around her waist and surreptitiously held her breast. Jencyn, watching from the alcove, hardened his face disapprovingly.

Catrin remembered the cold room on the hillside and the young man who lay there in feverish stupor. A twinge of guilt swept through her as she realised that since she had tended him she had not thought once of her father and brothers. Even now, the face that came most surely to her mind had the cleanly chiselled features and the fair skin of the fugitive. She desperately wanted to go back to the hillside. To bathe his brow to see if he needed any attention. She vowed that she would return before the day was out.

It wasn't possible. First, there were the geese to roast, and the Christmas dinner to serve, and although there were many hands, the maids were excited and needed a deal of supervision, and Jenette kept on disappearing with Dic.

"Let her be," Anne Thomas told Catrin finally. "Let her enjoy what life has to offer while she can."

Catrin looked at her mother in surprise, but this Christmas was certainly different. She recalled years past when she and rest of the family ate in state in the dining room in the new wing of the house, her mother aping the manners of the minor gentry, setting places with matching cutlery, drinking tea from a china cup.

Now, pretence torn away, they ate in the big farm kitchen, drawing support from the company, comfort from the farm gossip. Today, the ale flowed freely and the aroma of goose and plum pudding lingered around the rafters.

After dinner the carollers arrived together with Shoni with his harp, and Catrin found it impossible to slip away and ride back to the hillside. She did find time however to make a decoction of barley water as it was good to soothe a fever, and she prepared a dressing with charcoal powder for the man's wound. These she placed beside her bed together with some fresh linen for bandages and a large apple so that she could make use of one of Old Meg's magic remedies. She decided to leave the merry and somewhat reeling company downstairs early that evening, so that after a good night's rest, she could ride to the hillside before breakfast.

Jencyn also retired to bed early. He drank only as much ale as would quench his thirst, and watched in disgust as the other members of the household, and the visitors, drank their fill and more. Jenette, red-cheeked and merry, sat blatantly on Dic's lap and the couple kissed and cuddled in flagrant disregard of the company. Jencyn turned away from the depraved scene and climbing to his loft prayed loud and long for the young couple to recognise their sin.

27

Then he slept until Dic stumbled to his corner of the loft in the early hours and lay on his back, snoring. After that, Jencyn became only too aware of the sweaty, aley smell of the other man, of the occasional shuffle of the beasts beneath, of the scamper of mice, of the flurry of bats. Eventually he rose, and entered the kitchen just as Catrin was stepping in through the inner door.

"Don't you ever go to bed?" There was a touch of anger engendered by fear in the girl's voice. She wanted no one to know just how early she was leaving the house.

"I could ask you the same question."

Jencyn spoke evenly and stirred the fire into sparking life. Catrin flushed and drew her cloak around her to hide the provisions she had tied to her girdle. "This Christmas is difficult. You must know that."

She owed the man no explanations. He was a servant and so had no right to question her movements – and yet... she had to cover up. No one must suspect that a man was in hiding at the Holy Well.

"A canter on Sheba makes me feel better." She looked down at the stone-flagged floor as she spoke so that Jencyn would not see the anxiety and excitement in her eyes. "I'll be back for breakfast."

"I'll tell your mother. And I'll pray for you. God will show you His mercy if you hearken to Him and walk in His ways."

Catrin looked at him doubtfully as she left. The man was sincere, but his God demanded so much. Surely the curate too walked in the ways of God, yet he drank and made merry with his fellow men? She shrugged. Religion meant little to her. She had learned the Catechism and went to church on Communion Sunday, but she had felt no fervour or stirring of the spirit such as that which inspired Jencyn.

Today she left Bess behind. It was as well that the dog did not know her destination, lest she should innocently betray it to others. Although it was dark when she left, as she turned from the river and began the ascent along the winding, stony road over the mountain, the sky in the east lightened, and rosy fingers spread across the hilltop. There was little frost and Catrin was grateful that the weather continued so mild for the time of the year. Although at present bathed in a fever, the man would soon need to keep the cold at bay.

The path leading to the well lay beneath the bare, windswept summit of the hill and the way wound through silent, watchful oaks. Their stark branches provided little cover, but near the well a copse of holly and other evergreen bushes screened the girl and her horse from any inquisitive onlooker. She tethered Sheba and pushed open the ramshackle door. When her eyes became accustomed to the dim light, she saw that the man was lying in the same place as before, only now he raised himself on his good arm and looked at her unbelievingly.

Catrin dropped on her knees at his side and placed her hand on his brow, still hot, still sticky with beads of sweat. He relaxed and lay on his makeshift pillow.

"Are you real? Or are you some elfin creature come to mock me? I imagined that you came before, and at that time I thought that you were the statue of the Blessed Virgin come to life. Who are you? Tell me if you are real."

"My name is Catrin. I shall look after you."

"Then you are an angel, Catrin, and God will bless you. But why should you do this for me?"

Catrin began to unwind the now sticky bandage which covered the man's still swollen arm.

"I think, sir, that you should not talk so much. You are ill, very ill, but I have brought you something for your fever."

She cleansed the wound once more with the fast running water from the well, and bandaged the injured arm with the charcoal poultice next the skin. Then she lifted her flask to the man's lips, supporting his head and shoulders as she did so, as despite effort he was too weak to raise himself again.

"Barley water is all I could manage," she apologised, "but many say it is good for fever. I cannot bring you the expensive decoctions the doctor brought my brothers ..."

Her voice faltered and she shivered as the horror of that summer illness sprang back into her mind. She remembered the decoctions of snails, the powder of dried vipers, the blistering which had failed to control the confluent smallpox spots. She pulled the apple out of her bag and, peeling it, cut it into three pieces. Old Meg's magic was probably more effective than the doctor's repulsive remedies.

On the first piece of apple she carved the letters, D P. *"Deus Pater,"* she explained as she held it to the man's lips. "Eat it, sir. You shall have one piece a day while I say the magic words. *Deus Filius* for the second piece, *Deus Sanctus Spiritus* for the third piece. After that the fever will leave you."

"Those are holy words, but used in superstition. I am not sure that I should eat."

"Please do, sir. Old Meg's remedies rarely fail. Some say that she is a witch."

"I am too weak to argue and you have brought only good, little Catrin. But don't call me 'sir'. My name is Simon."

A faint flush spread over Catrin's face as she watched Simon eat. He stretched out his good hand and held hers and warm comfort sprang between them. The sudden chill that Catrin felt down her spine was due to emotion as much as to the cold dawn which now swept the hillside with grey light, but it reminded her that the building was cold and as well as medicaments Simon needed warmth. A few charred logs were piled on the floor as if he had made an attempt to light a fire when he had first arrived at the well.

"You have flints?"

"In my pack."

As Catrin gathered tinder together, Simon watched hazily, his thoughts drifting, unable to unravel reality and fantasy. A short while ago he had known Catrin to be real but now he was not sure. He was aware of his burning fever, of his hard bed, and now there was a bright flame nearby and a pile of logs and a soft dropped kiss on his forehead, which strangely brought peace amongst the frenzied pictures which tormented his mind.

One moment he was back in the churchyard at Preston where he had received his baptism of fire in fierce combat with King George's men. He remembered the desperate fighting, the unequal odds, and also the elation when things were going for his side. Then searing pain and the blackness of unconscious days. He recalled the blacksmith and his wife who had tended him and hidden him, who had risked their lives for him but who were anxious for him to leave as soon as he was able.

The nightmare trek south presented itself in sharply defined vignettes; bodies hanging from gibbets, groups of soldiers with muskets ruthlessly searching; the welcome haven of a friendly, probably Catholic house, with a further address to make for. His wound, though suppurating, gave him little trouble, until a fall on rocky ground near Brecon opened it again. Even so, he persuaded his last protectors, a middle-aged couple called Morris who lived near Merthyr Tydfil, that he was well enough to travel on.

"There may be a rising in the West," he had told them. "They will need all the help they can get."

The Morrises had tried to dissuade him. The West had failed to rise, they said. The expected support was not forthcoming. People were surprisingly accepting a German as their King.

"You should stay here until you are well," they told him. "Then leave the country as soon as possible."

But Simon wouldn't listen. So much was now at stake. His estates, his title, his way of life, his adherence to the Stuart cause, his Catholic faith. He had left Merthyr with the first signs of fever springing hot on his brow and had stumbled south across the ridgeway from Aberdare to Penrhys, blindly following the rough map Mr. Morris had prepared for him. When he felt that he could not travel another step, the small haven on the hillside appeared as a gift from the gods.

Now he had felt a kiss on his forehead. A kiss with its promise of love and care and affection. The memory comforted and helped banish the wild and frustrated pictures of recent happenings. It brought back remembrance of a time when life had been happy and free; when as a lad he had roamed his father's estate in Derbyshire, riding and hunting, but also making friends with the tenants and learning from them how to hedge and ditch, to sow and reap.

"You should have been a peasant," his father laughingly remarked more than once, and sometimes Simon, closeted with the chaplain, attending to his Latin studies, agreed with him.

Now, the memory of those carefree youthful days lulled him to forgetful sleep as Catrin untethered Sheba and retraced the path down the hillside.

She had been longer than she had anticipated and a flutter of nervousness disturbed her as she neared Ty Celyn. Today she feared more than before Jencyn's probing eye, but as she neared the farm she became fearfully aware of a noisy disturbance, of voices raised, of horses neighing and dogs barking.

She reined in Sheba and approached the farm gate cautiously. To her dismay, a red coated soldier stood guard outside and in the farmyard more soldiers, armed with muskets, probed and searched in the barns and outhouses.

Catrin's throat was dry with fear and she could scarcely find breath to reply to the questions the guardsman asked her roughly. Then a tall, immaculately dressed officer stepped from the farmhouse door and approached her. His cool eyes held a hint of amusement as he studied her flushed, windswept appearance, and his lips curved mockingly.

"The daughter of the house, evidently. Let her in. She has some explanations to give us."

THREE

The officer swaggered ahead of Catrin as if he was empowered with the lordship of the manor-farm. The girl, regarding him beneath cautious lids, felt indignation vie with her alarm as she picked her way across the mud and stones and followed him into the kitchen. The maids were huddled against the wall, ostensibly fearful, but giggling whenever one of the raw militia men approached. Jencyn sat near the hearth, silent and watchful. Catrin was aware of his close scrutiny as she crossed the stone-flagged floor. The officer beckoned her to the door leading to the living quarters of the house, and the girl, numb with apprehension, followed him to the dining room in the new wing.

A fire leapt and beckoned in the wide hearth, sending roaring sparks up the black chimney from the crackling wood, and throwing a warm, diffused glow over Anne Thomas who sat nearby. Her hands, tensely clasped in her lap, betrayed a fear which she resolutely kept from her features. Catrin met her eyes and the glance which passed between them was one of cautious dismay.

The officer sitting astride one of the dining chairs leaned his arms on its back and with a sardonic grin beckoned Catrin to take a seat.

"My name is Willoughby. Captain Willoughby.

As you may have gathered, my job is to grout out rebels, to dig out Jacobites, to stamp on any disaffection to his Majesty, King George."

A hot spot appeared on Catrin's cheeks. "In that case, sir, why do you bother to trouble us? Our loyalty is not in question."

"Yet you were known for many generations as being a recusant family."

"Not any more." Anne Thomas' face was stony and she spoke firmly. "You will find no Catholics hereabouts. Not since Philip Evans and John Lloyd were hanged and drawn in '79. If our rulers wanted to scare us then and fine us out of existence, they succeeded. We all will take the Oath and take the Test and keep our inheritances."

"I am delighted to hear it." There was a glitter of amusement in Captain Willoughby's cold, grey eyes as he turned his glance from daughter to mother. "Yet hearts are little changed in a mere thirty years. There has been seditious talk in the neighbourhood. Suggestions that Queen Anne willed the throne to her brother across the water but that the document was destroyed. Such talk," he added deliberately, "will be punished. The Lord Lieutenant of the County has called out the militia to make sure of everyone's allegiance."

"We are not interested in politics." Catrin broke in impulsively. "We want to be left in peace to farm our land,

And.... and…."

"And….?"

Catrin had intended to add, *to care for our loved ones.* The words died on her lips as she remembered

36

poignantly the loved ones who had died during the year. . . . "enjoy Christmastide," she finished lamely.

"You should manage that, m'dear." The Captain's eyes raked her mockingly, from the dark cloud of hair which tumbled over her shoulders and the soft fichu draped over firm, young breasts, to the mud-spattered hem of her homespun gown, and the riding boots, only partly concealed by her petticoats.

"I am told that you are in the habit of taking long, solitary rides across the hillsides."

Catrin's cheeks flamed. She was about to ask indignantly where the Captain had obtained this information when her mother broke in.

"My daughter hasn't been the same . . . neither of us has recovered from the deaths of my husband and sons. In the summer they died. From smallpox." Anne Thomas' voice faltered. "If Catrin can gain comfort from her lonely expeditions, I shall not stop her."

"Indeed, I would not wish you to. Your daughter may well be able to help us." Captain Willoughby turned towards the girl and looked at her piercingly. "I am sure that as she is such a loyal subject, she will tell us about any suspicious circumstances she might meet with in her travels."

"I cannot know what you have in mind."

"Why should you? But you may or may not know that there has been a rebellion in the North where the traitors to King George are waiting for James to land. The rising has been squashed and the ring-leaders, or most of them, are now in London where justice will be meted out to them. Others, lesser men, are hanging from gibbets to the delight of crows and all right-minded Christians. But a few are on the run, and we have had word that one of them is in this area. He was reported in Brecon and since then has made his way south, no doubt making for sympathisers in Ewenny or Kenfig."

"What will you do when you find him? Hang him?" Catrin's flushed cheeks had paled and she tried to will her throbbing pulse to some sort of calm.

"Not at all. We will send him to London to join his fellow nobles in the Tower or Newgate, where he will languish in fearful preparation for his sentence."

Catrin turned her eyes towards the fire. She did not want the Captain to recognise the horror and alarm which had sprung in their depths.

"So you would like to know if I have seen or heard anything which might lead you to him?"

"I can see that you are a sensible girl. You would of course be rewarded."

Catrin took a deep breath and faced her interrogator. Her nervousness dropped from her as a determined resolve grew inside her.

"I can assure you, sir, that I have seen nothing that could in any way give rise to alarm. But you have my word that I will bear your warnings in mind, and I shall remember the reward. A sum of money would be very useful to us in our present circumstances."

The Captain saw only a pair of candid eyes meeting his from an open, ingenuous face. He rose, his suspicions allayed, the edge of his aggression smoothed over, as he took his leave.

"I shall withdraw my men, Ma'am," he told Mrs. Thomas. "I must apologise for our intrusion, but you must realise that we have a duty to do." He turned to Catrin. "Good day to you. I am most relieved that you will cooperate with me. I hope that we may perchance meet again under more favourable circumstances."

Catrin bobbed a curtsey as he left, and she and her mother stood silently as they listened to his sharp orders in the kitchen and courtyard, and the bustle and tramp of his men as they assembled and marched through the farm gate. The stumping sounds died away and Anne Thomas sank into her chair, her cheeks ashen, her hands trembling.

Catrin placed a warm arm around her mother's shoulders.

"Thank God, they've gone at last. Sit awhile, mother, and I will see that someone brings you a mug of warm ale."

The kitchen was alive when Catrin reached it. The maids were jabbering with excitement and even Jencyn was animatedly discussing the visitation with Twm. Their smiles and words died away when Catrin approached, almost as if they feared what she might reveal.

"There is nothing to concern you," she said, sensing their alarm. "Captain Willoughby explained the reason for his visit. There has been a rising in the North of England and the authorities are making sure of our allegiance to King George."

"Theme's not real soldiers," broke in Twm. "Ivor, the blacksmith's son at Pansy, was one of them, and another I know comes from Llantrisant."

"They are the militia," Catrin explained. "The Lord Lieutenant has called them out for the emergency, but they are real enough while it lasts, and their muskets and ball are real too. I assured the Captain that we are all good subjects of the King."

Jencyn smirked. "I hope you said, *what-King.* A difference of opinion there is in some places."

"I pointed out that all we want to do is to live our lives in peace. Now it's time to get this place cleaned up. Jenette, take some warm ale to the Mistress, and the rest of you get round the house and see if any damage has been done. We want a tidy place for the visit of the *Mari Lwyd* this afternoon."

Catrin thanked God for the expected arrival of the traditional wassailers. After the bustle of setting the farmhouse to rights and serving dinner, the disrupting visit of the militia was forgotten when a group of men from the village gathered noisily outside, whooping and cat-calling with gusto. They carried the *Mari Lwyd,* the name given to the skull of a horse, draped in white and be-ribboned and decorated with flowers.

In the kitchen, the maids and men-servants waited tensely for the drumming on the door and the cries for admittance. Jenette, her mind distracted for a short while from Dic, threw a few nervous glances towards Catrin and her mother who stood near the inner door. White-faced and immobile, they tried not to think of those other years, those other Christmases, when Harry Thomas had answered the calls of the visitors with his impromptu verses, and Will and Evan had pretended to protect the household from the invaders with mock aggression. Now Twm replied to the sing-song appeals for admittance, but falteringly, with a loss for words likely to lose the farmhouse reputation.

Then to everyone's surprise, Jencyn took up the refrain. In a good tenor, he tossed replies back to the intruders, parrying their requests with sound argument and a certain wit. Catrin listened with subdued respect. The man was no fool, that was certain. She wished she could be as sure of his loyalty. If anyone had told the Captain of her frequent absences from the farmhouse, it was surely he.

Now the door was open and a flurry of the light rain that was falling spattered over the floor as the party entered the kitchen with ribald laughter at their mock battle. There was food and drink for all and Catrin and her mother shook themselves from their daze to chivvy the maids and welcome the guests.

"You did well, Jencyn." Catrin felt obliged to compliment the man on his performance. "I did not think you approved of merry-making."

"You are right, Mistress. Nevertheless, old habits die hard. The pity is when simple pleasures are abused and defiled."

"No great harm will be done here, tonight, Jencyn." Catrin spoke sharply, irritated by the man's self-righteous tone.

"I trust you are right, Mistress." Jencyn's voice was level, but he watched the gathering with distaste, as more and more ale was consumed and Shoni struck a merry tune on the harp to accompany a bawdy song. He moistened his lips as he watched Jenette and Dic. The girl's red cheeks, her full bosom threatening to spill from her tight bodice, excited him; when Dic's arm crept around her waist and his hand rested on the girl's breast, Jencyn was only able to subdue his own passion by recollecting the pangs of hell-fire which would surely await the offending couple. It was right to take a bride; hadn't Paul said, "Marry, or burn," but

41

evil it was to take such pleasure in sensuous delights which were surely the work of the devil.

Jencyn himself would marry one day. He prayed daily that when the time came he would find a God-fearing, dutiful spouse, but from his earliest days he had been disturbed that the female sex either shunned or mocked him. His conversion had at least shaped reason around their attitude. Good women were evidently hard to find, but in God's good time one would come his way.

A medley of feelings jostled inside Catrin as she mingled with the guests, making sure that they were well attended and lacked nothing in the way of food or drink. She parried the compliments and good wishes plied her automatically, while trying to make sense of the day's happenings. There was no doubt now that Simon was a much wanted man; that he was the nobleman sought so assiduously by Captain Willoughby. There was no doubt too that the immediate danger was past. The men had marched north, towards Blaenrhondda, and according to information gleaned by Mari who had spent some time in the hay loft with one of the militia men, their plan was to cut across the head of the valley and to turn south along the valley of the Rhondda Fach or the ridgeway at Aberdare.

"The men don't like this job," she had confided to Catrin. "They don't see why they should search the houses and farms of people who are just like themselves, and they want to get back home to their own jobs."

Catrin had listened with a certain relief, but however the militia men might feel, there was no mistaking the dedication of Captain Willoughby, or his skill and determination.

Nevertheless she had no intention of being intimidated. She was a woman of the *Blaenau;* a traditionally stubborn and intransigent people. Her own family claimed descent from Madoc, a son of Iestyn ap Gwrgant, that prince who had fought so fiercely against the Normans. Was it likely, she told herself angrily, that she would bow meekly to Captain Willoughby, with his English name and manners and speech?

So the next morning, and the morning after, she took the same road by the river and climbed the same track to the well, and although she was aware of Jencyn's watchful eyes as she left, she knew too that there was no danger of being followed. The loyalty of the rest of the household was without question, and any absence of Jencyn would be noted and commented on.

By the third day, and by the time the third portion of apple was consumed, Simon's fever had left him. Although he was weak, he could sit and tend the fire easily.

"You are a witch, little Kate," he told her, "and your magic works. I am beginning to wonder just how many spells you have put on me."

Catrin, pouring hot broth from a flask into a wooden bowl, felt a warm flush over her cheeks. She was aware that Simon's blue eyes were filled with admiration as he regarded her. They were kind eyes. Eyes which matched the ease of his features and the firm jaw line which, although not lacking courage, held also compassion.

"Let me help you."

Catrin held the bowl while Simon spooned the hot broth with his good hand. His injured arm was still painful, although the swelling had subsided and the angry flesh was now tempered.

While Simon ate, Catrin remained silent, but she knew that she had to warn him, to tell him that he was being sought."

"There were soldiers at the farmhouse," she began tentatively. "I said nothing earlier. I wanted you to get well."

"Catrin, you must not endanger yourself. I'll go. Weak as I am, I'll leave your territory. No harm must come to you, little Kate. You are a witch, but a saint too."

Simon attempted to rise to his feet, but weakness overcame him and he stumbled. Catrin caught him in her arms. She knelt and cradled his head on her breast, and felt the firm flesh of his shoulders beneath her fingertips as she clasped him tightly.

"You can't go. Not yet."

Catrin wanted to add "Not ever" as she gently lowered him on to his makeshift bed. His features had paled and the golden beard which now framed his face accentuated the hollows beneath his cheek bones. Catrin found herself touching the rough stubble, stroking the square line of his jaw.

Simon smiled apologetically. "I'll shave soon," he promised, but for a moment he held her hand there, close to his chin, and then turning his head slightly, pressed his lips against the palm of her hand.

Catrin felt her heart contract as she drew her arm away. She rose and busily attended to the fire.

"You must stay a few more days, and that's quite

definite."

The words tumbled hurriedly from her lips, as much to allay the awakening emotion which rocked through her as to persuade Simon. "When mother and I return from our visit to Mr. Evans, then we'll see how you are."

"Who is this Mr. Evans?"

"A neighbouring farmer. He has invited us to share his hospitality and we'll be staying at his house for one night. Tonight. Mr. Evans suggested that it would not be wise for us to undertake the return journey in the dark and the bad weather."

"And so, Mrs. Evans will be busy today, preparing food and airing beds, and generally making ready."

Catrin hesitated and turned her dark eyes away from Simon. "Mr. Evans is a widower. His sister, Judith, keeps his house."

Simon caught hold of her hand and pulled her towards him. "And I am already jealous! Say you'll spare me a thought as you enjoy his wine and welcome."

"Sir, your words are presumptious. But I will spare you a thought. For you will be lying in the cold and the dark, while we sit in comfort."

Catrin stood and drew her cloak tightly around her. "I brought you an extra supply of food as I shall be unable to visit you tomorrow." The girl's voice faltered, but she drew a deep breath as she stepped away from Simon and the ambience of warm light gifted by the glowing fire. "The following day . . . I shall bring you more food . . . and you may be well enough to travel."

She turned quickly and left the derelict building before Simon could surprise the look of desolation which Catrin knew had spread across her features at the thought of their parting. She rode back to Ty Celyn struggling with a welter of emotions, and as they made preparations for their visit to Ynysbedw, the home of Griffith Evans and his family, Anne Thomas looked anxiously at her daughter's pale face.

"You don't look fit enough to go visiting, Catrin."

"Don't worry. I'm fine."

"Jenette was ill this morning." A tinge of fear had crept into Anne Thomas' voice. "I don't like this mild, wet weather. It brings sickness."

"Jenette has been eating and drinking too much."

Catrin, anxious not to be interrogated further, pursued her mother with questions about their wardrobe, and Anne Thomas was easily deflected as she told the girl that they should wear their riding clothes, but that Jencyn would lead a packhorse bearing fine dresses for the evening, and also a good cheese for the kitchen and a couple of geese for the spit.

"I don't intend to go empty-handed."

Catrin noticed the tight set of her mother's lips and appreciated the woman's need for independence.

Later in the day, with Jencyn leading, and Jenette who was to attend them in the rear, the small party rode in single file along the rough track which led south along the river bank. Catrin wondered, as they jogged along, just how much power Griffith Evans had over their fortunes. To her chagrin, her mother steadfastly refused to involve her in any financial problems, preferring to rely on the advice of her bailiff.

Yet, Catrin thought, she could be of so much help, even if it was just giving words of reassurance. Griffith Evans was well known for his hard bargains. He had acquired many farmsteads by shady means, although Catrin did not anticipate that Ty Celyn was in any danger on this count.

The way was wet and muddy and in several places the turbulent river threatened to spill and swamp the path. The rain had cleared and the wind, veering in a north-easterly direction swept down the hillside, blowing their cloaks around their faces and hinting of snow. Jencyn, who was leading the way, stopped when they reached Pont Rhyd Tew. He pointed at the wooden bridge, now splintered, its flimsy structure battered and leaning drunkenly over the swollen water. On the other bank, the hamlet of Pandy straggled at the side of a better road.

"I had thought it a good idea to cross here," Jencyn told Mrs. Thomas. "The road is broader on the other bank and we could have crossed back at Cymmer. But as you see, even the ford is impassable."

Jenette shivered, as much with fright as with cold. "Mistress Catrin," she whimpered. "Can't we turn back?"

Anne Thomas, who had secretly been thinking the same thing as the path grew swampier and the air colder, now turned indignantly.

"Indeed, we cannot. Jencyn, lead on. We are all relying on you."

"There are but a few miles to go." Jencyn's eyes met Jenette's as he spoke and recognised hostility and dislike. He suppressed with anger the pang of hurt pride which swept through him. He continued suavely, "We will all rely on God. He will lead us into safe ways."

Whether or not as a result of Jencyn's faith and prayers, the party reached Ynysbedw as dusk was beginning to shroud the birch and hazel trees which framed the manor house. The dwelling was near the confluence of the two rivers, the Rhondda *Fawr* and the Rhondda *F ach,* the big and little Rhonddas, and its home lands were fertile, producing good crops and strong healthy cattle which fetched a good price in Llantrisant market.

Although the weather was bleak, Ynysbedw still presented a good picture, with a wide approach leading to a portico in the new style and square windows faced with stone. In summer, Catrin thought, the place would hold great beauty and no doubt the table would often be graced with salmon and trout from the nearby rivers.

For the time being she was glad to have arrived. Jencyn, with help from a man-servant, led the horses to the stables as the door opened and Judith Evans welcomed Catrin and her mother. They stepped into an oak panelled hall, liberally decorated with Christmas greenery. A fire blazed in the wide hearth and Catrin stepped towards it gratefully, holding out her pinched fingers to its comforting warmth.

"I'll show you to your room. Your servant can bring your things."

Judith Evans, thin and spare, led the way up the oak treads of the staircase to a room in the front of the house.

"I expect you will want to change from your

ridingclothes." The woman's voice was dull. She sucked in her pale cheeks as she spoke and her eyes flitted uneasily around the room, rarely meeting the gaze of her guests. "Come down when you are ready."

Catrin looked around with some awe. By local standards the room was sumptuously furnished. Two standing bedsteads were comfortably equipped with feather beds and quilted covers. A great oak cupboard, ornately carved, stretched across one wall and as well as several stools, a frame table stood near the window and carried a large Bible printed, Catrin noted, in English.

Jenette bustled into the room bearing their clothing and the two women changed from their mud-spattered outdoor garments. Anne Thomas wore purple coloured silk and dressed her hair high under a lace frilled cap. Catrin thought how distinguished her mother looked as she followed her down the broad staircase. She herself wore a blue gown, basqued over a flower-sprigged petticoat. The frilled cuff of her best chemise emerged from her close-fitting sleeves, and her hair was dressed with a nosegay of lace and ribands, brought back by her father a year ago from one of his rare visits to Pen-y-Bont.

A maid-servant met them at the foot of the stairs. "The mistress says you are to go into the parlour. The company is waiting there."

Anne Thomas looked at her daughter cautiously. They had not expected other guests, but Catrin felt relieved. The purpose of Griffith Evans' invitation had bothered her; she had been sure that he must have some motive in asking them to stay, but now she was reassured. He was merely offering traditional hospitality to neighbours and acquaintances.

The maid opened a door and stood aside for the two women to enter the parlour. By the side of the fire, his fleshy features reddened by the flames, Griffith Evans sat corpulently, the buttons on his embroidered waistcoat straining across his girth. Morgan Howell the curate sat at the table, the light from a candle in a brass holder mellowing the powder on his wig. Standing near the hearth, the firelight glinting on the polished leather of his expensive boots, was Captain Willoughby.

Catrin subdued a gasp as she recognised him, and she sensed too, her mother's alarm. Her feeling of reassurance left her as she entered the room and the Captain's mocking eyes met hers.

"A pleasant surprise." Captain Willoughby bowed low. "I would have wished for such a meeting, but had not hoped that it would occur so soon."

Griffith Evans rose to his feet. "So you know each other," he mumbled with some irritation.

"Only in an official capacity."

"Captain Willoughby searched our farmhouse some days ago," Catrin broke in bluntly.

Mr. Howell coughed in embarrassment. "Routine, of course. I'm sure that Captain Willoughby did not relish that task."

"We have many unpleasant duties to perform, but often there are compensations."

Catrin turned from the Captain's unnerving stare. A deep fear had begun to well up inside her. The hours they were to spend at Ynysbedw would, she knew, be fraught with danger.

FOUR

Catrin was glad when Judith Evans announced that the meal was ready for conversation at the table was less likely to take a compromising turn, but she was dismayed when Captain Willoughby offered her his arm. It was impossible to refuse, so with fast beating heart Catrin allowed herself to be led into the long dining room, and found herself sandwiched between the Captain and the parson. Griffith Evans sat at the head of the table, flanked on one side by his sister and on the other by Anne Thomas. The other member of the party was Herbert, Griffith Evans' twelve year old son, who sat at table with dismal eyes and was soundly cuffed each time he made a remark in Welsh.

Anne Thomas' eyes swept enviously over the table as she entered the room. It was made of heavy oak, with intricately carved legs and claw feet and Catrin, intercepting the covetous glance, knew how much her mother had wanted to replace their own trestle and board with a similar piece of furniture. Today the table was graced with a damask cloth, and places laid each with a fork, knife and spoon, and a silver goblet. Griffith Evans filled these at once with a clear golden wine he told the company had been brought over especially from France by the importers in Bristol.

Mr. Howell's face creased in warm benevolence

as he lifted his glass. His living was poor and he intended to enjoy to the utmost the lavish hospitality which was being offered to him.

"Nadolig Llawen!" he toasted in a moment of forgetfulness.

"Merry Christmas!" countered Mr. Evans with a curl of his fleshy lips.

"Merry Christmas!"

"Merry Christmas!"

Even Judith Evans managed a wan smile as glasses were raised and the first wine of the evening sipped. Then the servants carried in platters of Christmas fare; a boar's head, roast goose, chickens, a Christmas pie containing pigeon, partridge, hare and woodcock. Later there was plum pudding and syllabub made from strong beer with the froth of warm milk added straight from the cow, and plump currants strewn across the surface.

In spite of her anxiety, Catrin enjoyed her meal and managed to steer the Captain's conversation towards innocuous channels. It was not difficult as Captain Willoughby was in the mood to forget his mission for a few hours and to enjoy a harmless dalliance with a pretty girl. As compliments and pretty speeches flowed from his lips, his flattery overcame her caution, and Catrin's cheeks flushed with pleasure. Once or twice she noticed her mother glancing at her with some concern and she intercepted too, curious glances from Griffith Evans, but these latter held more than a trace of annoyance.

"Captain Willoughby, Mistress Catrin, help yourselves to more syllabub, and while you are at it, perhaps you can join in the general conversation. We are losing the obvious wit of your remarks."

Griffith Evans spooned a large helping of plum pudding on to his platter as he spoke. His eyes glared stonily at the younger man. He had no wish to alienate Captain Willoughby. Indeed his aim was quite the opposite; the Captain had contacts with many of the gentry with whom Evans was anxious to establish cordial relations. Nevertheless he had brought these Thomas women here for a purpose, and he could not bear to see this purpose thwarted.

The fact was, Griffith Evans had two great needs which he was determined to meet. One was for more children. His two wives, besides adding their property to his, had brought him many offspring, but Herbert was his only surviving child, and he was so sickly that his father feared that another hard winter would pluck him away to join his brothers. Besides the boy did not have the stamina or spirit Griffith expected to see in a son. His second need was for a bed-mate. Griffith was a lusty man and had already learned the dangers of dallying with the maid-servants. One, a simple minded girl. had been sent back, pregnant and weeping to her parents; another, more devious and cunning, had proved difficult, presuming on her relationship, but Griffith was not a man to stand nonsense. The girl had been sent packing to seek her fortune elsewhere.

The Thomas women now ... Griffith's lips curled sensuously as he studied the curves of Anne Thomas' full breasts. A lot could be said for a woman with experience, and Anne looked the sort who would know how to please a man. The girl excited him more. He watched her now as she daintily pecked at the syllabub, her dark eyes merry with laughter at the Captain's jests, her glossy hair curling down the soft creamy line of her neck. She was a beauty was Catrin, and likely to bear sons, but the mother was the one who held the property. Although mortgaged to him to the hilt, Griffith Evans hesitated to foreclose and annexe the farm in that way. Such an action was likely to damage his already tarnished reputation with the people who mattered in the county. No, far better to marry the little widow and gain Ty Celyn in an acceptable fashion.

"Have you completed your business in the neighbourhood, Captain Willoughby?"

Griffith Evans' voice boomed across the table, commanding attention.

"Very nearly. Just one little matter more."

"I know of no disaffection in my flock, Captain." Morgan Howell coughed apologetically in an attempt to exonerate his parishioners.

"Have they any affection for anything, Vicar?" The Captain's eyes flashed sardonically. "Surely their besetting sin is apathy? But I am not so concerned with your little flock as with those outside it."

"You'll find no Papists here. Dissenters in plenty, the more's the pity, but they are hardly likely to espouse the Jacobite cause."

"Welshmen are likely to espouse any cause in order to harass the English. Particularly up here in the *Blaenau* among the hill people. They have a stubborn reputation."

"But you have found nothing suspicious." Catrin forced her voice to steadiness although her fingers clenched with alarm and her throat was suddenly dry and parched.

"That is true. And we will be withdrawing to Cardiff and the Vale after just one more small foray. Tomorrow at dawn, we go to search a ruined hospice which we missed at our first visit."

"You mean Penrhys, Captain," Evans broke in. "I have plans of the place. You must see them later."

Catrin paled in horror. The rest of the evening was a nightmare. She spoke, smiled, laughed, automatically. She reacted to the Captain's advances with over enthusiasm in an attempt to hide her despair and anxiety.

Her mother watched Catrin's frivolous display with growing alarm. "I think we'll retire early," she said at last with a warning look at her daughter. "We had a tiring journey today, and tomorrow we have to brave the wind and the mud again."

"You are wise, Ma'am." The Captain bowed. "I too will take my leave of the company, as tomorrow promises to be an active day for me also."

As Catrin mounted the stairs to the room she was to share with her mother, a plan was evolving in her mind. A wild, desperate plan, but if she did nothing, tomorrow Simon would be caught, trapped in the niche she had made habitable for him. He would be carted off to London ignominiously and there ... she shuddered as she contemplated his fate. Simon himself had no illusions. "If they get me they will hang me," he had told her several times.

"They will not get him." Catrin repeated the words over and over to herself as she lay in the comfortable bed and waited for the deep breathing

which would indicate her mother's sleep. Her plan would work ... must work.

As soon as she was sure that Mrs. Thomas was sleeping, Catrin slipped from the bed and put on her riding clothes. Her fingers trembled and fumbled over the fastenings, but finally, her boots in her hand and her cloak thrown over her shoulders, she tip-toed from the room and down to the kitchen. A glow from the hearth lit her way to the door which led to the courtyard behind. Although Catrin had not been to the outbuildings before, the needs of the household, although grander, differed little from those of Ty Celyn and she had no difficulty in finding the stable.

Here it was darker and the building was long and housed many animals.

"Sheba," she whispered. "Sheba."

She paused as a low whinny led her to the mare. The horse nosed her affectionately, and Catrin undid the low gate of the stall and slipped a bridle over the horse's head. She ignored the saddle. The side-saddle which she normally used was cumbersome and difficult to buckle on the horse. Catrin had ridden wildly across the hills since she was a small child and she decided that tonight she would ride astride the horse, bareback. That way she would gain more speed. Her heart beat fast as she mounted the animal and guided him away from the house, choosing the muddier stretches in order to avoid the clatter of hooves on cobbles.

To her relief, they left the estate without detection, and sheltered by the dark cover of a holly grove, found the track which led alongside the river. Catrin was grateful to the moon which lit her way and helped her to avoid the more obvious hazards. The wind had dropped and a hard crust of frost was forming on the surface of the muddy tract. As she passed Penrhys, Catrin glanced upwards towards the little well, as if with willpower she could see through the maze of branch and twig and evergreen to the rough bed where Simon lay.

"I'll be with you soon, Simon," she breathed. "I'll save you, never fear."

She rode on, for her immediate goal was not Simon's hiding place but her own farmhouse. She realised that it would prove too great a task to move Simon by herself. She had to have help and as Jencyn ap Dafydd was safely ensconced in Ynysbedw there would be no problem in recruiting aid.

Reaching the farmhouse, she tethered Sheba to the gate. Then she ran across the yard to the kitchen door. The room was deserted except for Bess, who at the intrusion sprang to attention. On recognising her mistress, the dog subsided sleepily on to the warm stones near the hearth, wagging her tail in welcome.

Catrin crossed to the door leading to the cow shed and opening it, called softly, "Dic! Dic!"

Dic, alone in the loft, was a few moments stirring. Sleepily he peered down the ladder.

"It's me, Dic. Catrin Thomas. I need help."

Dic fumbled around in the hay for his breeches and pulling them on joined Catrin on the floor below.

"What is it, Mistress?"

"Sssh! Quiet Dic! We don't want to wake the household. Can I trust you?"

"Of course, Mistress. You know I'd do anything

for you or Mistress Thomas."

"I want to hide someone in the old barn with no questions asked. Will you help?"

"Just tell me what you want me to do."

"Get two horses, one for you and one for the stranger, and come with me."

Dic, alert now, and excited by the adventure, pulled on his coat and quietly saddled a couple of horses. Then he followed Catrin along the river track and up the mountain, until they stood outside the old well.

"What we are doing is very dangerous, do you understand, Dic? You must tell no one. Not even Jenette."

"You can rely on me, Mistress Catrin."

Although only twenty, Dic was a big man with a shock of red, curly hair and an ingenuous smile. Catrin knew she had taken a risk. If Dic betrayed his knowledge it would be through his naivete, for his loyalty was sound. The risk had to be taken. Simon was surely lost otherwise.

Inside the building, the fugitive slept beside the dying embers of the fire. Catrin ran inside and clutched his arm. "Wake up, Simon. Wake quickly."

Simon stood, immediately wary; on the defensive when he saw Dic enter the building behind Catrin.

"You have to leave, Simon. At once. Dic here will show you to a place of safety, Take all your things." Catrin paused and touched Simon's cheeks with her fingertips. "I have to go now. God be with you. I will see you as soon as I can."

She turned on her heel making for the door, but

Simon put out his arms and drew her towards him.

"You can't go just like that. Catrin, do you know that you are risking your life, or at the very least, transportation? Please think again."

Catrin felt the man's fingers press into her flesh. His breath was warm on her cheek as he spoke.

"There is no need for me to involve you or any of your household: I'll make my own way, Catrin*."*

"And get yourself arrested!" Catrin turned on him angrily. "I've come all this way for you, and this is all that you can suggest?"

"I do not wish that you should get into trouble."

"I'm in it already. Up to my neck. But you are to do what I say, Lord Simon Nichol. I know what's going on around here, and I know too, how best you can reach safety."

A slow grin spread over Simon's face. He stood, tall beside Catrin, and placed a hand on her head.

"Mistress Five-foot Nothing," he smiled. "And yet I, erstwhile nobleman and landowner, have to do just what she says."

He dropped a featherlight kiss on Catrin's forehead and the girl felt her body melt inside her. She stepped away from him.

"I have to go. Dic, you know what to do?"

Dic was already collecting Simon's effects, his platter and cup, his maps and kerchief, and pushing them into the pack. As the girl left she saw him help Simon struggle into his greatcoat.

A good hour was needed before dawn as Catrin descended the hillside and retraced the trail to Cymmer. The frost was biting now, and if the mud beneath the crust of ice on the path had not been yet soft enough to cushion the horse's hooves as the slippery surface cracked and splintered, the way would have indeed been treacherous. But Catrin was relieved to find that she could yet make good speed. She entered the courtyard at Ynysbedw with some trepidation, anxiously peering through the shadows in case she should be spied. Apparently the whole house, master, mistress, guests and servants slept deeply, and Catrin threw a blanket over Sheba in the stable and re-entered the house, relieved that her activities were unnoticed.

She was unaware as she passed through the kitchen that crouched in the ingle-nook, frustrated by the sleeplessness that constantly dogged him, Jencyn huddled near the low flames seeking warmth. He started in surprise when the door opened and Catrin entered the room. In the dim light shed by the glowing hearth, he noticed her flushed face and the tenseness of her expression. He was about to stand and challenge her when some caution advised him to remain unseen, and he watched silently as she pulled off her boots and tip-toed through the door which led to the main hall and the stairway.

When she reached her bed-chamber, Catrin undid the fastening on her bodice with fingers numb with apprehension as well as with cold. Her riding habit slipped from her shoulders and clad only in her chemise, she climbed between the bed-clothes, shivering at their icy texture, but warm inside with relief at the success of her venture.

Her complacency was short-lived.

"Catrin!"

Her mother sat up in the adjoining bed, and in the pale light creeping through the window, Catrin could see the look of accusation on the other woman's face.

"How could you, Catrin! I was sufficiently disturbed last night by your behaviour with that man, but this! You are not a servant girl. What I can excuse in Jenette, I cannot accept from you."

Catrin lay back on the pillows, shaken and mortified. So her mother thought she had spent the night in Captain Willoughby's bed!

"It's not what you think, mother," she excused herself lamely.

"Rubbish, girl. I am old enough to know a lecher when I see one, and I could see the flattery he was pouring over you last night and the way you played up to him too. But this! Have you no thought for your position or your future?"

"Truly, it's not what you think," Catrin pleaded. "I can't explain. Not now at any rate. Please say nothing of this to anyone, mother."

"What do you take me for, girl? A fool. You may rest assured that your night's activities will never be mentioned by me. I only hope that the fancy Captain has sufficient respect and honour to do likewise."

In spite of her anxiety, Catrin was sufficiently exhausted to sleep fitfully until it was time to rise. Jenette came into the room to put out the women's clothes and help them with the awkward fastenings and her eyebrows lifted in surprise when she noticed Catrin's green dress lying in disarray on the floor.

"I swear I put it away for you," the girl protested. Her cheeks were pale and she put a hand to her mouth as she swayed slightly.

"Aren't you well, Jenette?" Catrin sprang from her bed to support the other girl, but Jenette clung to the bedpost and attempted a smile.

"I'm fine, Mistress Catrin." She stooped to pick the green dress from the floor but Anne Thomas caught her by the elbow and drew her upright, gazing suspiciously into the girl's wan face as she did so.

"Are you ... ?" The woman's lips damped shut as she saw Jenette's eyes flare with fright. She released her hold of the girl's arm. "Go downstairs," she ordered. "Get yourself a cup of ale. We'll manage here and you can come up later to pack for us."

Jenette escaped speedily and Catrin dressed in silence, avoiding the stony glances her mother afforded her. Judith Evans met them as they descended the stairs and led them to the dining room where a large fire was already flaring in the hearth and a breakfast of hot butter-milk and bread and cheese awaited them.

Herbert sat at the table munching at a hunk of bread *"Bore da!"* he greeted the visitors, in Welsh now that his father was not nearby, and then lapsed into a fit of coughing.

"A bad cough he has had for two months or more," his aunt said anxiously, and Anne Thomas noted the high spot of colour in the centre of each of the boy's ashen cheeks. The lad was not long for this world if she was not mistaken. She had seen too many children go the same way. Griffith Evans would be looking for a young wife, she thought with a pang.

As a person the man held no attraction for her, but the previous day she had coveted the fine table and chairs, the linen, the silver and the pewter, and intercepting the man's sensuous glances she had realised that both she and her daughter were being regarded with speculation. The implication of a match did not escape her. It would be the end to worry over the mortgage if she was the chosen prize. But Mr. Evans would surely need a younger partner. At thirty eight, she had not yet passed the child-bearing stage, but the chances of her daughter providing the man with an heir were surely greater. She threw a despairing glance at Catrin. The girl was demurely sipping at the butter-milk, just as if, thought Anne Thomas, she had not tried to throw away her chance of a fortune by getting implicated with Captain Willoughby.

"The Captain made an early start," Judith announced as if she had followed the trend of her visitor's thoughts. Catrin looked sharply at her mother and noticed the way her mouth had hardened into a tight line. "His men were bedded down in the barns, but they have all moved off now. Perhaps they will catch their quarry this time."

"Rubbish! They are on a wild goose chase. There are no Jacobites in this neighbourhood." Anne Thomas spoke from conviction and Catrin, keeping well out of the conversation as she toyed with her bread and cheese, was glad that she had not taken her mother into her confidence.

"You may well be right." Judith Evans sighed and picked up her knitting. She was working at a long, grey stocking, as colourless as her features and her opinions, which had been washed away by a lifetime of agreeing with her brother.

"We must make an early start, mother." Catrin

felt that she could not bear any delay. She had to get back to Ty Celyn, to see Dic, to know that Simon was indeed safe in the barn.

To her delight Judith agreed. "Our chief waggoner says that snow is on the way," she told them "The wind is blowing hard from the North-East once again, so you would be wise to be off soon. My brother is in the parlour. You may take your leave of him there."

The two women put on their cloaks and made sure that Jenette and Jencyn had the horses and the luggage ready before they paid their respects to their host.

Griffith Evans sat near the hearth smoking a tapering clay pipe. He was dressed in a long, oriental silk gown and as he had not put on his full wig, his shaved head was covered with a close-fitting embroidered cap. Catrin suppressed a smile at the incongruity of such delicate linen head-gear surmounting Griffith's heavy, florid features. The man arose, his big frame towering over the two small-boned women. He held Catrin's hand just a fraction too long, and then did the same for her mother.

"We have enjoyed our visit, Mr. Evans." Anne Thomas told him, "but all good things come to an end, and now we must leave."

"We will meet again soon." The man's eyes roved from one woman to the other as he wondered how to play fortune against youth. "Very soon, I hope."

Outside, Catrin and her mother found Jenette taking care of the horses. "Jencyn has gone inside for a moment," she told them as the wind buffeted their

64

cloaks against their faces.

"We will wait in the porch." Anne Thomas looked around in annoyance but it was not long before Jencyn joined them.

Catrin, noticing the slight curve of his lips and the sharp glances he threw at her from his almond shaped eyes as he helped her mount her horse, shivered slightly with alarm. As quickly, she threw her fears to the wind. What could Jencyn do that would harm her or Simon? He knew nothing.

As their small trail wound down to the river bank, Catrin found elation raise her spirits. Each step brought her nearer to Simon, and reminded her of the success of her overnight plan.

She may not have felt so complacent if she had known that it had been Griffith Evans who had called Jencyn back to the house as they were about to leave. He had pressed a coin into the man's hand.

"You are an intelligent man, Jencyn," he had whispered hoarsely. "Keep your eyes open and your mouth shut. I'll see you in a month and you shall tell me what goes on at Ty Celyn."

"Such as ... ?"

"How can I say? That's your job. There will be more in it for you if you do the job properly. Any snippets of information will help me make up my mind about a certain problem."

Jencyn hesitated. There was plenty to tell already, but perhaps the time was not ripe.

"Rely on me, Mr. Evans," he said as he went to join the others. "I can be very discreet."

As they pressed on, leaning against the bitter

wind, he pondered on his unexpected task. A sense of awe began to pervade him. Perhaps he, Jencyn, was being given his chance. Griffith Evans was a powerful man, a rich man, and Jencyn's prayers for fortune had been fervent. The Thomas women would only suffer by his disclosures if they failed to walk in the way of the Lord. The Lord looked after His children and rewarded good living.

And Jencyn, riding forward with frozen fingers and chilled flesh where the wind tore through the worn places in his suit, knew with certainty that reward would one day be his.

FIVE

The wind cut across the farmyard like a scythe when the travellers arrived at Ty Celyn, the horses bowing their heads against the blast, the women's skirts and cloaks tossed around their knees, the bare, iced branches of the trees straining and groaning as they genuflected beneath the onslaught. Twm, a sheepskin across his shoulders, hurried to greet them and to lead the mounts to warmth and shelter. He was accompanied by Rhys, the odd job man, and Catrin felt a stab of alarm when she realised that Dic was nowhere to be seen.

"Snow there is in this wind," the old man commented as he took Sheba's reins. "The bite I have felt since dawn." He gazed lugubriously at the leaden sky which encapsulated the valley and robbed the hills of their summits. "Dic is out with the other lads to bring down the sheep and cattle to lower pastures."

"Good man, Twm." Anne Thomas entered the kitchen with relief at the man's forethought. Decisions which had always been made by Harry were being forgotten this winter.

Jencyn built up the fire and looked slyly at his mistress." We must hope that the animals are brought safely down in time," he said. "I told Twm weeks ago that this should be done. Although the weather has been mild, we should have anticipated this change."

Anne Thomas looked at him coldly. "I have every confidence in Twm. He worked with the master for many years. Bring us broth, Jenette," she ordered irritably. "We need something to drive away the cold."

Catrin noticed how Jenette's face had dropped when she heard that Dic was not on the farm. The girl now helped Mari serve the hot food, but although bustling around the warm kitchen, her cheeks were pale and her lips drawn into a tense line.

"Do you think they will be long out there, Mistress Catrin?" she whispered as she served the bacon broth. "The weather is not fit for a dog to be out, particularly on the hills. "

"They'll be back soon." In spite of her reassuring words, Catrin's heart pounded unmercifully. Had Dic accomplished his mission? Was Simon safely hidden in the old barn at the end of M*aes Glas,* the green meadow? Her anxiety mounted as the hours passed, and by the time Dic returned frozen and hungry, in the early afternoon, she felt feverish with the tension. Even then, there was difficulty in obtaining the information she waited for. The man was famished and the serving maids surrounded him, reviving him with food and drink. Jenette too, clung to his side, and finally Catrin had to risk suspicion and order the shepherd to the parlour where she could question him privately.

"Everything is as you wish, Mistress," the young man told her. "I've put the stranger in the old barn with food and a lantern. He won't be disturbed there, particularly now with the weather turned bad."

"Thank you, Dic. Go back to Jenette. I know she's waiting for you."

Catrin managed a smile, but in spite of her relief she now burned with determination to get a flask of hot soup to Simon. A fire was an impossibility in the barn, and with the temperature dropping every moment, Simon would surely perish with the cold unless he had plenty of good food.

Filling a flask from the great *crochan* which steamed with the bacon broth it contained, was fairly simple. Catrin merely waited until the maids were busy in the buttery and the men were attending to the animals. Leaving the house unseen was more of a problem. She would have to go before dusk but she would surely be seen if she wandered through the yard. She decided to leave through the front door of the house, rarely used at this time of the year, and breathed a sigh of relief when she found that it opened easily and without creaks.

Maes Glas was a good half mile away and the going was rough, with the wind buffeting her, tearing at her cloak and tossing her hair about her face. The fields seemed endless, grey in the dying light, and peopled with alarming shapes which reminded Catrin fearfully of the ghostly tales told around the fire on such wild nights. Catrin stubbornly put her fears behind her as she scratched her way through hedges and climbed over the obstacles which the wind had thrown in her path.

The barn, when she reached it, was sheltered by a projection of rock on the hillside, and so protected from the full fury of the wind. She found Simon huddled beneath his greatcoat and reading by the flickering light of the lantern. Rather, he was attempting to read, for since his arrival at the barn,

Simon had been at the mercy of several conflicting emotions. His anxiety to get away was balanced by an ever increasing desire for Catrin's presence, a desire which minimised the discomfort of his surroundings.

He dropped his book when Catrin entered and held his arms towards her. As she flung her head on his shoulder, his lips touched her soft hair, and a strange feeling, unrecognisable from any previous experience grew inside him. Simon was a man, and he wanted to possess Catrin as he had possessed women before, those idle women of society whose aim in life was to seduce or be seduced, but now his feelings were mingled with something deeper. The wish to protect, to serve, the desire to keep Catrin to himself always.

These feelings were foolish. Under normal circumstances, he could have nothing to do with a girl like Catrin. It would be his duty to find a wife of noble blood. A Catholic girl who could help him preserve the faith his family, or most of it, had suffered for for so long. Now he was on the run. His future a questionmark. This was not the time for dalliance either of a frivolous kind or for discovering deeper feelings. And yet ...

He held Catrin at arm's length. "You should not have come in this bitter weather. I did not expect it. Did not Dic tell you that I was safe and well?"

"I had to see for myself. And to bring you this."

"Bless you, Catrin." Simon accepted the flask of broth great fully . "I have made up my mind. I intend to leave tomorrow. No ... "He held Catrin's hand as she was about to protest. "I am quite determined. You have been put in sufficient danger on my account already. My arm is improved and I shall leave at dawn. For London, for I am sufficiently convinced that the rising in the West has not taken place. If I go to the capital, I shall find out what has happened to the cause and those who fought for it."

"You will be running into danger.... "

"I have no option. But do not worry, sweet Kate. I shall take no unnecessary risks."

"And I shall see you no more ... "There was a hint of desolation in Catrin's voice, a pleading which caught at Simon's throat and set his veins on fire. He drew her towards him and twining his fingers in her dusky hair, pressed his mouth on hers. He wanted to take her, to lose the memory of his danger, of his bleak future, in an oblivion of love and passion, but he put the girl tenderly away from him. Catrin was no courtesan. Even had she been a mere serving-wench, Simon had been taught by his chaplain to resist the temptation of despoiling the underprivileged. But Catrin was more than he had ever hoped to find in a woman. He gazed at her now in the flickering light of the lantern, at her haze of hair, the soft roundness of her cheeks, her well-proportioned frame, small yet determined, and the blood pounded in his veins with love and longing.

"Goodbye, Simon." Catrin almost sobbed the words as she turned and fled from the barn. She almost welcomed the hammering of the wind as she left the shelter of the building, for fighting with the elements as she ploughed her way back to the farmhouse, helped to blunt the edge of her desolation. The dusk had deepened now to a grey dark, and as Ty Celyn hove into view, snow-flakes flailed around

Catrin's head, and driven by the wind, whipped around her heels.

She gained the door with relief, and pushing it behind her, leaned panting against it to regain her breath. Suddenly she was aware that her mother stood in the hall, her back stiff as a ramrod, bewildered disapproval written on her face.

"What are you up to, Catrin?" she demanded angrily. "I insist that you tell me."

"Don't ask me, mother. Just trust me." Catrin hesitated, then ran up the stairs to her room where she shook the snow-flakes from her cloak and then abandoned herself to a fit of weeping. Simon was going! At dawn tomorrow, he would leave her life, perhaps forget about her for,ever. How would he be able to remember her when he was fraught with danger on all sides? But she would never be able to forget him. Catrin knew that as surely as if it was written in the Bible in the parlour. Simon had come into her life, and in a few short days had transformed it. The months ahead beckoned in a desolate sequence. Bereft of father and brothers, they had previously seemed formidable enough. Now hungry for her lover, Catrin did not know how she would bear the lonely days. And there would be no one else. Not ever!

The wind tossed open one of the small windows, and chased a gust of snow into the room. Catrin was obliged to leave her black reverie to fasten it and as she did so saw the raging blizzard outside, she caught her breath with rising elation. She remembered a storm like this three years previously. Then, morning had shown an arctic world, with drifts ten feet deep, and isolating them from their neighbours for days on end. If this should happen again, Simon could not possibly leave.

Even as her spirits rose, a black thought crept to her mind to disturb her. How would Simon survive with no fire, no comforts, with only his coat to provide an inadequate cover from the penetrating cold?

Catrin left her room and joined the household downstairs, her mind alert and racing. She had successfully foiled Captain Willoughby in his attempt to capture Simon. Now, somehow, she had to evolve a plan to bring Simon into the safety and warmth of the farmhouse.

Her mother was agitated and not even the merry laughter in the kitchen, dispelled the tension on her face. Shoni, the harpist, and Griff, the dancer, had come to visit before the onslaught of snow had driven all the hands and servants to the shelter of the kitchen, and now they sang and made up verses, seemingly oblivious to the wild elements which bruised the walls and the doors and spattered the windows with meteoric showers of snow.

Catrin tossed her head and met her mother's eyes challengingly. The woman approached her.

"I was wrong last night, Catrin. Forgive me for my unjust accusations. You had been out in the night hadn't you?"

The girl looked at her mother warily. "And if I had . . .?"

"Things have been too much for you. Perhaps when the weather improves, we will get Dr. Johns over from Llantrisant to give you a draught. Meantime I shall make a decoction of horse-radish and you must rest. Promise me that you will rest."

Catrin's eyes opened wide with amazement, but with relief also. So her mother suspected nothing more than that she was suffering from a form of madness!

"Don't worry about me, mother. I'll do what you say."

Anne Thomas, mollified to some extent, sat in the chair which had once been Harry's and tried to enjoy the limpid music which flowed from Shoni's expert fingers. The maids were full of excitement, chattering like sparrows - except Jenette who sat silently near Dic. Their faces were solemn, in contrast to the lively vivacity which had sustained them only a week ago. Not only Catrin and her mother, but Jencyn too, noticed this fact, and his heart stirred self-righteously. The Lord was already wreaking His vengeance, thought Jencyn, and he prayed again that the couple would realise their evil ways and repent. He stirred uncomfortably, as he found that he was praying only for Jenette. Dic, he could not have cared less about.

The storm outside showed no signs of abating, and it was not long before Shoni and Griff realised that they would have to stay in Ty Celyn, for the night at least. The idea caused a great deal of merriment, with Griff chasing Mari around the kitchen, until Mrs. Thomas' poker face put an end to their horseplay.

Anne Thomas retired to bed complacently, thinking that at least Catrin was safe that night. She could not possibly wander around outside in such conditions, and the woman resolved that she would do all she could on the morrow, to keep the girl occupied and safe from brooding. Perhaps it was partly her own fault, she thought accusingly. Her own grief had dulled her susceptibilities to the needs of her household and then there was her pain . . . A twinge now caused Anne to double up momentarily. She would ask Dr. Johns' advice about this too, when he came to visit Catrin. She lay down and slept soundly, exhausted by the morning's ride, the weather, the tensions.

In the adjoining room, Catrin, still clad in her homespun gown, with an extra shawl thrown around her shoulders to keep the cold at bay, sat near the window and prayed for the storm to abate. Lying on the floor was a pile of clothes, taken by her from the huge chest at the top of the stairs; Will's *"dillad cig rhost"*, his best Sunday clothes. Sober clothes of dark grey and black braid, the kind of clothes any country gentleman would wear for travelling. Sufficiently undistinguished to be unrecognisable by anyone who had not seen them for a length of time. As the hours passed, Catrin thought she detected some abatement of the wind. The flurries of snow thrown against the window grew sparser, and Catrin opened it to find the world outside blanketed in white drifts and the gale reduced to a gentle sough in the branches.

She threw on her cloak and tying the clothes on the floor into a tight bundle, left her room and crept silently to the front door. She gasped with dismay as she stepped into a deep drift, but Catrin was not easily thwarted. She soon found, by the light of the moon which had found a break in the overhanging cloud, that the snow had piled in drifts on the northern sides of the hedges, leaving a gap which was relatively clear. Even so, the going was difficult, and Catrin wondered what sort of a trail she was leaving behind her in the tell-tale snow.

She found Simon in the barn with his bag packed, waiting patiently for the first rays of dawn.

"You'll get nowhere in this," she exclaimed. "The tracks will be covered, you'll perish in the drifts."

"The storm has died away," Simon argued. "It can't be all that difficult."

"I've been out in it and I know." Catrin tossed the bundle of clothes on the hay. "Here, take these."

Simon stopped and picked them up. He examined the dull cloth, so different from his own richly embroidered vest and waistcoat. "Do these encompass another of your plans?" There was a hint of tender amusement in his voice as he spoke.

"This will work, Simon. Just like my last plan. You must change into these clothes and walk out for a while in the snow. Then you must pretend to come across our farmhouse by chance and seek refuge there. My mother has never turned anyone away yet."

"And who shall I say I am?" Simon asked quizzically. "That's up to you. You will know more about these things than I. You will know the sort of person likely to be abroad in the countryside."

At first Simon was dubious. Then his face lightened. "I could be a cartographer. That's it, Catrin. It is high time a new map was made of these parts. Perhaps we can make this work. At least we'll know that if the weather prevents me leaving, Captain Willoughby will not be able to seek me either. By the time he is able to search, I shall be far away and no one could blame you for taking in a mysterious stranger under these conditions."

"Leave your own clothes under the hay," Catrin

advised. "I can collect them later."

Before leaving, she touched his hands gently. Simon stooped over her. He did not repeat his passionate kiss, but dropped a warm, grateful caress on her forehead.

"God bless you, Catrin. I am glad our leave-taking is delayed for a few days."

Simon's words revolved in her head as Catrin made her way back to the farmhouse, making light the difficulties of walking through the snow-covered fields. The moon was covered once more, and again the wind had begun to howl. A few eddies of snow whirled in the air. Catrin was glad that she knew the fields so well. Once or twice she stumbled into deep drifts that engulfed her to the waist, but she extricated herself and tried to ignore the eerie overhead sound of ice burdened, snow-dressed twigs, as they scraped and twisted together.

By the time she reached the haven of her room, her dress and cloak were sodden. She shivered as she found herself another shift and crept into bed. She would ask Jenette to dry her clothes discreetly. As she had another homespun dress, her mother need not suspect that she had been out. Catrin fell asleep exhausted, and did not wake until Jenette came into her room with washing water.

"Why, Mistress Catrin," she exclaimed. "Your dress and your cloak!"

"Jenette, you must dry them for me. Quietly, you understand? Don't let the Mistress see them. Will you help me?"

Jenette's eyes opened wide but she nodded. "Of course, Mistress Catrin. I'll take them now, and I promise you no one will know."

The girl left the room, and Catrin thought once again that the serving-maid's face looked drawn and pale. She felt a fever of excitement however as she dressed, and had no time to ponder over Jenette's problems. There was a sparkle in her eyes as she descended the stairs, and she did justice to her good breakfast in the busy kitchen. Her mother was already up and she looked at Catrin's rosy cheeks with relief. The girl looked so much better today. Perhaps she was being overanxious about her behaviour. Harry had always complained that she fussed.

Shoni and Griff were eating their fill, together with the farm hands. "Looks like we're here for a bit, Mrs. Thomas," Shoni said, with little regret in his voice. "Bad as ever, now it is."

Catrin looked anxiously through the window at the driving snow. She felt concerned for Simon struggling towards the farm. She hoped desperately that he didn't lose his way in the blizzard. The one advantage of the weather was that he would be genuinely in need of shelter and sustenance when he arrived.

The men gathered in a corner of the room to play dice to while away a few hours. All that is, except Jencyn who watched them mournfully, and Dic, who sat at Jenette's side. Now the young couple rose and sidled up to Mrs. Thomas, and the shepherd cleared his throat purposefully.

"We would like a word with you, if you please, Mistress."

Anne Thomas noticed Jenette's grey face. "You'd better come into the parlour," she said drily. "You come too, Catrin. This is bound to concern you."

She sat in the big chair next to the blazing hearth with Catrin standing behind her, and looked at the young couple who stood sheepishly before her.

"I think I know what you have to tell me," she said. "It is not the first time the story has been told, nor will it be the last. I want to know what you intend to do about it?"

Dic's mouth opened but his throat was dry and no words came. He turned apologetically towards Jenette, who caught his hand with a sudden gesture and replied impulsively. "I love Dic, Mistress, and Dic loves me. We want to be married."

"But you are not in a position to get married."

"We were thinking ... " Jenette hesitated, then meeting Catrin's sympathetic glance went on more confidently. "There's an old cottage down by the water-mill. Falling down it is, but Dic will do it up. And I'll go on working for you until ... until I have the baby. Then I will help at the harvests and at all the other times when you need extra hands."

"So, you've got it all worked out. But you didn't think of all this when you acted so foolishly did you?"

"Please, Mistress. We couldn't help what we did. We just couldn't help it. And we won't be a trouble if you let us have the cottage. We'll help, and our children will help too."

Anne Thomas' face softened. Her heart went out to the young couple standing before her. So young. So hopeful. So unaware of the great tragedies and disappointments which awaited them in life.

"Be happy while you can," she said gently. "Of

course you can have the cottage. And you shall have the bidding in the farm kitchen. If Dic gets on with what has to be done to the cottage, the villagers will fill it with what you need to set up house."

"Oh, thank you, Mistress Thomas," Jenette wanted to throw her arms around the woman's neck. She caught hold of Dic's hand instead. "Let's go and tell everyone. They will want to drink our health."

The two left the room with shining faces and Anne Thomas rose and placed her hand on Catrin's arm. "Jenette is lucky." she said. "In different circumstances, the girl might have been out of the house to fend for herself."

The babble of noise in the kitchen rose to a crescendo as the couple broadcast their news. Catrin and her mother smiled at the sound of the merriment and laughter which filled the whole house. Then the noise died away suddenly and Catrin, instinctively knowing why, clutched fearfully at the pendant which hung around her throat.

"What can have happened?" Anne Thomas threw open the parlour door in curiosity and surprised Mari who was hurrying towards them in excitement.

"Mistress Thomas, it is a traveller ... in all this snow! He has come to ask for shelter."

Behind her, standing framed in the doorway, stood Simon. Catrin tried to stem the pounding in her veins, and attempted to conceal the light of recognition in her eyes.

Dressed in a flowing black cape and the sober grey suit, and with a snow-speckled wig covering his fair curly hair, Simon had lost his look of youthful candour , and had stepped into the part of learned traveller in the manner born.

He bowed low to Mrs. Thomas. "Simon Johnson, Ma'am," he introduced himself, using his mother's maiden name. "I have lost my way and my luggage. I crave your hospitality until the weather becomes more clement."

"Mercy on us all," Anne Thomas touched his cloak and the greatcoat which was sodden to the waist. "Of course you must stay. Catrin go and find the gentleman some clothes from the chest on the landing. These will have to be dried off."

She led Simon into the parlour and as Catrin ran up the stairs she turned and saw Simon's blue eyes gaze at her with love. Her cheeks were red with excitement as she opened the oak chest. Her second plan had worked, even to the extent of Simon needing her brother's clothes!

SIX

For three days the farm remained completely isolated, with intermittent falls of snow piling again on the drifts. The men of the household were strained to the limit, searching for buried sheep and bringing them to the comparative shelter of the copses and thickets near the house. Mrs. Thomas was relieved that Shoni and Griff were there to help, and Simon too gave his assistance unstintingly. They returned to the kitchen, cold, wet and hungry but the pot was always boiling and filled with *cawl,* a nourishing leek soup, and there was salt beef and pork and plenty of bacon, to keep the devil out.

Mrs. Thomas looked at Simon apologetically as he sat near the hearth, a bowl of broth cupped in his hands, his breeches and coat steaming from the heat of the fire.

"You should be eating in the parlour, Mr. Johnson," she told him, "and as for going out with the men, I am grateful, but do not expect it of a gentleman."

"Think nothing of it." Simon smiled at her candidly. "The truth is, I enjoy hard physical labour. When I was a boy, I used to escape lessons and join the men in the fields whenever I could. My father always said I should have been a peasant. He could not see me ever making a . . . gentleman."

Simon hesitated as he had been going to use the term "nobleman", but recollected himself in time. For moment his mind slewed back to those halcyon days when the sun always seemed to shine and there was haymaking, and welldressing, and the time-worn rites of harvest. A way of life that he wished could go on forever, envelop him completely, but there had been another side - the side of duty, the Latin studies, the sword-play, his travels in Europe, his meeting with the true King, James III. Life at the court of St. Germaine had not attracted him. He was too active to welcome the sycophantic life of the courtier and when he had news of his father's death, he was only too glad to go home to claim his inheritance. He remembered now the shock of finding his uncle's family ensconced in the Hall, the feeling of betrayal when he discovered that they had all conformed, were attending the Parish Church, had taken the "Test", that is, they had received Communion from the Vicar.

"You want to lie low for a bit, lad," his uncle had told him. "That is, until we see how the land lies. You know the rules of inheritance as well as I do, and unless you are prepared to take the Oath and the Test, you may as well consider the Hall lost. I'll take over for a while until we see what is happening. That way we will be able to keep the horses."

His uncle spoke logically. By dint of laws passed by William of Orange, all Catholics were made incapable of purchasing or inheriting lands, and also were not allowed to possess a horse of the value of £S or more. These laws Simon knew would be repealed when Queen Anne died and King James III came to take possession of his rightful throne. But now it seemed the country had accepted German George, and Simon's future was in shreds.

He tore his mind away from his recollections and attended to his food. He was not a man to brood on misfortune; if he had learned anything from his travels it was to be self-reliant, adaptable, and to accept what life had to offer gratefully. He knew that he was attracted to Catrin in a way he had never before felt for any woman. The girl possessed so delicate a beauty - and so sturdy a spirit. There was an affinity between them which could offer a mutual strength throughout life. He met Catrin's gaze now and felt refreshed by the consideration he saw there. Yet, how hopeless it all seemed. Were he still a nobleman there would be barriers between them which determination might well surmount. But as he was, or appeared to be, penniless, homeless, with an army seeking him out for retribution, he could offer nothing. He pushed aside his bowl impatiently. He must get to London as soon as possible to find out if the Jacobite cause still had any hope of success.

Catrin noticed the gesture and also saw the man stride impatiently to the window. She stood behind him and followed his gaze as he looked out to the white yard with its glacial water butts and paths piled with iced crystals. Now the sun appeared briefly, picking out prisms of colour as its rays danced over the frigid surface.

"Do you want to leave us so much?"

As Catrin spoke Simon turned round and if the maids had not been bustling around with the clothes for drying, and Catrin's mother had not been sitting knitting beside the fire, he would have taken her in his

85

arms and been tempted to pledge his love to her for a lifetime.

"I would wish these days to last forever," he told her in a low voice. "But unfortunately nothing can be solved if I stay."

All the same, he found many moments when he blessed the white blanket outside which kept him prisoner at Ty Celyn. After some days, a slight thaw reduced the drifts so that Shoni and Griff could make their way back to the hamlet across the river, but the track down the valley was still blocked.

However it was now possible for Jenette and Dic to get in touch with Morgan the Mill who was also the *Gwahoddwr,* or Bidder. Mrs. Thomas had advised them to arrange the wedding without any delay and Dic had dug his way to the old cottage, braving the snow drifts, and had decided that by dint of hard work and the promised help of the other hands, he could make it habitable in a fortnight. So Morgan put on his tall hat, tied a white ribbon in the button-hole of his coat, took his Bidder's staff, with the fine ribands flowing around it, and with a bag on his back to collect the offerings of bread and cheese which he expected to receive at the farmhouses and cottages he visited, made his rounds, reciting impromptu verses. Dic ap Eynon and Jenette Jones were to be married, he announced, and a dinner would be given for them by the kindness of Mrs. Thomas Ty Celyn, who had offered good beef and cabbage, mutton, pork and potatoes, a quart of drink and a cake. Attendance was requested with a good song and what they could afford to give; jugs, basins, pots, pans, platters and dishes, a sack of flour or a child's cradle.

Jenette lost the wan, haggard look which had dogged her, and excitement and happiness made her cheeks glow and helped her to overcome the nausea which often coloured the dawn of her day. Catrin gave her a bunch of coloured ribbons to put in her hair, and Jencyn watching the frivolous display felt his faith in the justice of God shake ominously. How was it that these two, so blatant in their levity and wrong-doing, were apparently prospering? He, Jencyn, would be left to his solitary nights in the hay loft, while Dic was to be given the comfort of a cottage and a family. Jencyn prayed long and fervently that these things would be explained to him. Perhaps, he thought, he was being punished because his thoughts of Jenette had often been lustful, and he asked God to strengthen him, to help him put away these lewd ideas so that he could walk in righteousness.

Catrin, hearing the excitement in Jenette's voice as the maid chattered to her about the coming change in her status, and bringing Dic's name into each sentence a dozen times, wished that her own position could be as simple. If only she and Simon were ordinary country folk, with the same chance of happiness as Jenette and Dic. Then, her own tongue would repeat Simon's name a hundred times a day! As it was, she must be thankful that the snow was clearing only slowly, and that the bite in the wintry air promised no let-up in the frosts.

"Can you not stay until Jenette's wedding?"

Catrin and Simon had escaped from the farm for a short while. The sun sparkled from an ice blue sky and although the ground was anvil hard beneath their feet, they were able to climb the hillside surely, avoiding the drifts and the obvious patches of ice. The wind, less angry but still cold, had whipped a fine colour into Catrin's cheeks, and her dark eyes danced as she confronted Simon. They reached a copse of holly and hazel and paused, sheltered by the evergreens, and by a boulder which robbed them of the full force of the wind. From their position they saw the valley spreading beneath them, from north to south an expanse of white waste, with here and there smoke rising from the chimney stack of a cottage or farmhouse which merged into the landscape by dint of whitewashed walls. The black branches of the trees had shaken free from their burden of snow, and their gaunt, hungry shapes etched dark patterns on the alabaster vista.

"It would appear that I have little choice but to stay." Simon's lips curved as he answered Catrin's question, and his candid eyes met her tenderly.

"Not necessarily. The wind could change. In a day or two, we may well be back to our usual rain or sleet, with mud underfoot instead of ice."

"Unlikely. The witch of the North-East has already given us a week together. She is likely enough to cast her spell for a week longer. But I will stay for Jenette's wedding, dear Kate, even if the sun should jump in the sky and summer surprise us." Simon's arms held Catrin close and his fingers tightened on her shoulders. The holly behind the couple was rimed with frost, ice on the rock beside them draped like frozen tears. "I would that we were simple cottagers like Dic and Jenette. There are so many barriers between us, yet all I want is to be with you, Catrin. I would build for you, sow for you, reap for you, garner the harvest, hew the wood, draw the water."

"And I would work also for you. I would make sure you had good food. I would spin the wool, weave the cloth, tend the fire."

Simon's lips met hers, at first tenderly then with growing passion until she pushed him from her angrily.

"What are these barriers?" she demanded impetuously. "Why cannot you stay with us at Ty Celyn? Why can we not marry and have you run the farm? We need a man, Simon. I need you."

"Because, my darling, Captain Willoughby and his men would be down on us like a hive of bees and as well as spiriting me away, your future and the fate of all in Ty Celyn would be in ribbons. And that is why I must not tarry. The longer I stay, the more likely I am to bring trouble to your home."

Silently, the couple descended the icy paths and the sun chose that moment to sink into a gathering cloud.

"We'll return past the old barn," Catrin suggested. "It is not safe to leave your things there for anyone to find."

They collected Simon's embroidered coat, his waistcoat, his fine lace cravats and his sword, and Catrin picked up from the straw the braid Simon had torn from his tricorne hat and the tell-tale cockade he had worn on its side.

"You should burn that," he advised her, but she shook her head.

"I shall always keep it," she told him. "I'll hide it safely. No one will find it."

An old flour sack lay in the corner and Simon piled his clothes inside and then slung it over his shoulder.

"There can be many explanations if we are questioned," he told Catrin, but in fact, they returned to the farm unobserved. Catrin took the sack when they reached the upper storey and going into her room opened the lid of her chest.

The oak chest was a new one, made especially for her eighteenth birthday. The initials C. T. were carved on the front, encompassed by a motif of vine-leaves and flanked by the date, 1715. The wood was bright and smelt new and inside was Catrin's wardrobe; her silk dress and her riding habit, her shifts and lace kerchiefs, her ribbons and the nose-gays and treasures she had collected over the years.

Simon's clothes and his sword went underneath, well camouflaged by the linen and the garments above, and Catrin once more marvelled at the way Simon had been able to disguise his identity. Her mother had betrayed no trace of suspicion, but had apparently accepted Simon's story without question.

Catrin was being over-complacent, lulled into a sense of false security by her own wishful thinking. Her mother was no fool, and in spite of the excitement engendered by Simon's arrival, she had not failed to notice that Catrin was tense rather than curious, or that when the girl's hand touched the stranger's the two exchanged a quickly suppressed, but warm glance of recognition. Many facts began to slot into place in Anne Thomas' mind and although Simon's garb initially aroused no suspicion in her mind, her notions led her to examine his clothes more thoroughly as they were set out drying near the hearth. There was no doubt in her mind as she ran her hand over the rough fabric that it had been spun, dyed and woven on their own farm.

At first anger had suffused her. How could Catrin be so stupid! The man was evidently the Jacobite sought by Captain Willoughby and his men, and the girl had connived at his escape. Her tongue was ready to lash her daughter with furious recriminations and she was for turning Simon out in spite of the snow. Then the alarm which inspired her wrath also cautioned her. She decided to say nothing. Her ignorance was the family's best defence, and her heart even contracted with compassion as the days passed and she watched Catrin and Simon so happy in each other's company.

She played her part well. In the evenings the three sat in the parlour, and Simon at the table, his wig lending him an air of learning, pored over old maps which had once belonged to Harry Thomas.

"You must tell me about your work, Mr. Johnson," Anne Thomas enquired politely.

Catrin, unnerved, shot Simon an alarmed glance, but the man smiled suavely.

"There is little to tell, except that it is high time a reliable map was made of this area. The strip maps of the main roads are useful to the traveller but they leave out much of value."

"Then your work will be sought after." Anne Thomas smiled and was tempted to tell the young man that she knew why he was so interested in maps. But although caution bade her hold her tongue, she had a few pertinent words to say to Catrin later, when they were alone.

"Have you thought about your future?" she asked the girl bluntly.

Catrin looked startled, then her lips tightened. "I suppose you mean marriage."

"What else could I mean? You will inherit the farm one day, so your dowry will be a good one."

"This means that I am to be bartered like a score of cattle or a hundred sheep."

"What else is there for us? I was lucky with your father. We loved each other, but marriage is necessarily a business." She paused. "You must have realised that there was a purpose in Mr. Evans' invitation."

Catrin's eyes flashed in horror. Griffith Evans' suggestive glances had certainly not escaped her.

"Mother, I could never . . ."

"Rest easy, Catrin. I'm pretty sure that I, myself, am the prize."

"But do you want ...?"

"It is not a question of what I want. Rather of what is necessary. You know yourself that we cannot run this farm without help. We are already in debt to Evans and a couple of bad harvests could ruin us. Besides, there are compensations. All my life I have wanted good things. Silver instead of pewter, glass instead of wood. I've wanted fashionable clothes and to mix with the gentry and to serve salmon and trout on a real table, not just a board and trestle."

"And this is what you would get as your part of the bargain?"

"I'm not forgetting you, Catrin. The farm will

belong to Mr. Evans should I marry him, but there will be a marriage settlement. I shall make sure that a good sum will be settled on you when you wed. Your future will be assured, but only if you play your part." She looked at her daughter keenly, pleadingly. "You must be circumspect in all that you do. No breath of suspicion of any kind must attach to you."

A hot spot appeared in each of Catrin's cheeks and she turned from her mother, unable to meet her gaze.

"There was nothing between me and Captain Willoughby. I swear it."

"And I believe you. But I have seen the way you look sometimes at Mr. Johnson. Be careful, Catrin. Let your head rule your heart." She put a restraining hand on Catrin's arm as if to emphasise her point.

"You don't have to worry." A bitter smile played around Catrin's mouth as she replied. "Mr. Johnson will be gone soon. And I will very likely never see him again."

Nevertheless, Simon had promised to stay until the wedding, and before that, there was the football game. This was to be held on Sunday morning in the churchyard, weather permitting, and anxious eyes were turned to the sky for a sight of the rain clouds which would bring a thaw. Dic was the star player of the Llanfodwg parish. His height and broad shoulders gave him a distinct advantage over the other slighter, shorter men, and this time he was determined to score more points than ever before. He was to be married on the following Tuesday, the day chosen by Jenette, as folk wed on a Tuesday would be sure to have a lifetime of good luck and happiness. So it was important that he should shine in the game, for his sake, and for that of his bride. On Saturday a slight drizzle made Dic's eyes light with pleasure. The opposing team would be able to reach them after all.

Catrin's feelings were less happy as she watched the white banks disintegrate and disappear into grey pools. The icicles hanging in pristine splendour from the eaves slowly dripped away and the talk among the men on the farm was of the coming battle, and how the Llanfodwg men were going to give their opponents from Llantwit a good licking.

On Sunday morning, Jenette was lively with excitement, and she wound in her hair the coloured ribbons Catrin had given her. "Watch, I shall, from this side of the river," she told the household, most of whom intended to join her.

Simon looked inquiringly at Catrin. "May I join you in witnessing this sport?"

"Of course. We have to stay over on this bank," she explained. "No one knows what will happen during the game. It is safer to keep well away."

The only sour note was sounded by Jencyn. Since the announcement of Jenette and Dic's marriage he had remained morosely aloof from his fellows, sloughed in a deep depression. Now, as the other servants made ready to leave for the game, chivvying Dic with lewd comments and indulging in excited horseplay, he felt constrained to protest.

"This wickedness will be punished," he admonished them. "Sabbath breakers are you. Know you, that you must keep God's commandments. Keep Holy the Sabbath Day."

One of the farm hands made a rude sign and Mari burst into peals of laughter. "Who do you think you are then Mister self-righteous Jencyn? And who do you think is going to take any notice of your miserable ideas?"

She flounced after the others leaving Jencyn in the kitchen, pale and shaking. He sat down to read his Bible and prayed that God would soothe the unreasonable mortification he felt. He did not relish being unpopular.

Tension was already beginning to spring in the air around the old church. Morning service over, the handful of worshippers left the building and the hens, scratching around on the green, scrambled away from the assembling players and sought refuge under the benches inside. The game, in theory, was played on the north side of the church, that part of the graveyard where no burials took place, but as everyone knew, the play was likely to move anywhere. The Llantwit players had arrived some time before, regaling themselves from the large flasks of ale they carried and were already merry and full of fighting spirit and singing songs of battle. The Llanfodwg men countered with their own team cries, and Dic, swigging a great draught of beer, rallied his men with a bellowing chant.

"Will we beat them?"

"Aye, we will!"

The ball was put into play and Simon, watching from the other side of the foaming river, found it difficult to assess what exactly the players intended to achieve. One moment they were in a turbulent, flailing mass rolling in the mud, then with a cry a player would kick the ball away and the men would follow to repeat the process in a different part of the churchyard. After ten minutes, one man had retired with a twisted ankle and another had found himself immersed in the Rhondda river. The ground was slippery with treacherous pockets of ice and snow, but Dic could be seen in the thick of every tussle, his red hair flaming angry messages at his opponents.

Jenette watched him proudly as his thick-set shoulders stood out among the other players. Then the teams, oblivious of the curate's admonishments about broken tombstones, moved around the church. The pace was growing, the spectators cries rising in a crescendo, the players scrabbling, fighting, and pushing, sometimes for no apparent' reason except that a Llantwit man had come face to face with an inhabitant of Llanfodwg.

"Where's Dic? Get them, Dic." Jenette's voice was taut with excitement and for a moment she did not think that there was anything sinister in the fact that Dic was nowhere to be seen.

The cries changed, subtly, so that at first those on the opposite bank did not realise that anything was wrong. The play stopped; the ball rolled inside the forked roots of a yew, forgotten, abandoned. A man with red hair lay sprawled across a tombstone.

"Dic! Dic!"

Jenette shrieked as she flew across the bridge. Simon and Catrin followed closely but when they arrived there was nothing they could do to help.

Jenette cradled Dic's head in her lap, her eyes wild with shock, gasping her lover's name as he breathed his last, his back broken from the press of men who had twisted him against a headstone.

SEVEN

Dic was buried two days later on the day that he and Jenette were to have wed; the day that had been set aside for the bidding.

During the night he had lain in the kitchen in a coffin hastily made by Owen the Brook, woodturner, with two candles at his head, and two at his feet and a pewter plate of salt on his breast to keep away the evil. The men from the village, his team-mates, his fellow hands at Ty Celyn, had assembled to keep watch for the night. One by one they had stood beside the plain oak casket and had muttered the Lord's prayer before congregating round the hearth. The hot spiced ale provided by Mrs. Thomas went some way towards dispelling the chill from the window, left open for the freedom of the dead man's soul. Perhaps because of the manner and suddenness of Dic's departure, or because of his remembered popularity and goodwill, or because of his youth, there was less levity than was usual at such *agwylos* or wake, but nevertheless the kitchen was warm with the hum of voices which often during the long hours erupted into song.

The accident had sent Jenette into a state of shock. On the morning of the funeral she went about her early morning household tasks, silent and white-faced. Catrin, remembering her own desolation at the funerals of her brothers and her father, caught the girl's hands compassionately.

"It passes. Believe me, Jenette, the worst of the grief passes."

The servant looked at her mistress with drowned eyes. "And what about me, Mistress Catrin? What will become of me?" The girl paused and sobs began to shake her frame. "Whatever is to become of me? A baby I am having, and no husband to look after me."

Catrin drew in her breath sharply. She herself had been so distressed by Dic's death that she had not considered the full implications of Jenette's predicament.

"Perhaps the parish Vestry. . . ."

"A lot of good they did for Mary Morgan. A shilling shroud she had and another for her baby."

The chill of fear which drained the girl's face was almost tangible. Catrin could find no words of comfort, but later she spoke to her mother.

Anne Thomas' lips tightened. "There can be no place for Jenette at Ty Celyn." She looked away from her daughter evasively. She was hard only because life had shaped her that way; had taught her to fight for her own; had shown her that thought for others was a luxury only to be enjoyed by the very rich or the very poor. "She has a mother, no doubt. Let her go back to her own parish. They must look after her there." Her mouth softened a little as she saw the distress on Catrin's face. "I'll see that she has the *arian rhaw,* the spade money," she added.

At the funeral the parish clerk held a shovel over the open grave and one by one the mourners came forward and placed a coin upon it, for the most part pennies, but here and there a shilling. Even a five shilling piece from Mrs. Thomas, in spite of the fact that she was to pay Owen y Nant for the coffin. When it was added up, there was ten shillings for Jenette to put in her pocket, and she accepted it quietly, dry-eyed, her shawl pulled tightly around her shoulders as if to insulate her from the frightening barbs of society.

Catrin left the churchyard with Simon, and as before, on Christmas night, she felt a reluctance to return to the farmhouse.

"This is your last day with us, Simon. Let us take horses and ride."

Simon agreed and Catrin found herself re-tracing the trail she had taken when she had stumbled on the secret of the old well.

"I thought you were bringing me here." Simon dismounted when they reached Ffynnon Fair and entering the small building, looked around at the bleak walls. The hard, earthen floor was still littered with the charred remains of the fire which had warmed the damp air; the trickle of water ran, as it had done for centuries, in the gulley along one of the walls. "I could have perished ... would have perished if you had not chanced along with your spells and your firm faith in my recovery."

"So why do you have to go away now and endanger your life once again?"

Simon cupped Catrin's face in his hands. "Kate, I love your eyes when they sparkle so spiritedly."

"For your own good!" Catrin broke away from him, her desperation turning to anger. "Why London? You will be putting your head in a noose!"

"Not so." Simon's lips curved as he shook his

101

head. "How little you know of the world, Catrin. London is the easiest place in which to lose oneself. Here, I stick out like a Maypole on a summer's day. I don't doubt that the balladmongers are already singing about the stranger who sought refuge from the snow at Ty Celyn, and the danger will be when they also sing of Captain Willoughby's fruitless search, and perhaps put two and two together. No, Catrin, I can endanger you and your household no longer."

He put out his arms to draw the girl close, but Catrin, alarmed by her conflicting emotions, the growing desire for Simon's love which threatened to overcome caution, the bitterness she felt over their inevitable parting, the desolation experienced at the funeral and its aftermath, ran out of the building and mounted Sheba.

"Let's go up to the top," she suggested, and Simon followed her along the stony path, up and away from the oak trees and hazel groves, the copses of holly and evergreens, until they reached the summit. Here, patches of snow still clung to the sparse, coarse grass and sat in pockets among the piles of grey stones which were all that could be seen of the hospice and chapel, once the goal of hundreds of pilgrims.

Catrin led the way along the ridge of the mountain until they stood a thousand feet up and the hillside descended at their feet towards the saddle-back of Llantrisant Common. Further on they could see the shoulder of the cairn topped Garth and beyond, the small port of Cardiff and the glitter of water in the Bristol Channel. This was the horizon of Catrin's world and one which she had explored only fractionally. Until now she had thought only rarely of what lay beyond, but now she realised that there lay Simon's world. She looked at the man by her side, hungrily, longingly, wanting to be part of that world. To stay by his side always.

"Take me with you, Simon."

"I want to." His voice was low and urgent. "God alone knows how much I need you, but for the present we have to part. I want to marry you, Catrin, but there are so many barriers. There is my faith ...."

"I care not a fig for religion, Simon, but your faith was the faith of my great grand-parents. I love you and I may come to love your religion too; but I can make no promises."

"I promise you this, Catrin. I'll take no unnecessary risks, and I will be back. Believe me."

They journeyed back to Ty Celyn in silence, negotiating the steep descent into the valley and surrounded by encompassing hills that today enclosed them, held them close, but that on the morrow would isolate them, throwing a massive physical barrier in their path. Catrin shied from the thought of the miles which would separate them when Simon was in London, although her lover assured her that many of those miles were not as impenetrable as the *Blaenau* country. Where the hillside met the flatter, kinder land of the plain there were roads broad and stable enough for wagons and carts to carry their wares, and coaches plied between the larger towns, sometimes at breakneck speeds.

The practical details of Simon's journey occupied his attention when they arrived back at Ty Celyn. Mrs. Thomas wondered how he would make his way without his luggage and without a horse.

"Take one of ours,' she offered. "You can send money back to us by a drover if you haven't enough with you. And keep the clothes. Little use they are to us now," she added. Her face relaxed. She felt a great relief that the man was going. Each day she noticed that he and Catrin grew closer to each other, so the sooner he was gone the better. The girl might break her heart for a while, but the hard facts of life would bring home to her the fact that she had to look elsewhere for a husband.

"Will you be long in finishing your map, Mr. Johnson?" Anne Thomas looked at Simon without guile although she had to suppress a twinkle in her eye as she did so.

"Long enough. I shall be travelling north towards Neath." This was the story that Simon had decided to tell to cover his tracks and by perusing the maps lent him by his hostess, he had discovered that he could take the northern track up the valley and then cut east, across to Gwent.

In the morning he was up at dawn, and accompanied by Jencyn who had been deployed to travel with him for a few miles along the river, left the farmyard riding a good black mare. Catrin, watching from her bedroom window, felt loneliness shroud her. She was filled with foreboding. Would she ever see Simon again? What fate awaited him in London? Was he walking into a trap? When Jenette entered the room bringing her washing water, she was too dispirited to talk, even to attempt to chivvy the servant out of the overwhelming gloom which had enveloped her since Dic's accident.

"Shall I tie the red ribands in your hair, Mistress

Catrin?" Jenette spoke unsmilingly and Catrin noticed that she no longer wore her own hair curled, but had pushed it inside her plain linen cap.

"Where are the ribands I gave to you, Jenette? Wear them. They will help give you a brave face."

The girl shook her head. "No more will I wear ribands. Punishment, that's what has been sent to me. Jencyn is right, I am thinking. Dic and me, we were displeasing to God."

"No Jenette. That can't be so!"

"Then why . . .? Stay here I can until Easter. That is what your mother says. Then, it's back home."

Jenette stuck her chin out a little defiantly. She wouldn't tell Catrin what this was in the way of punishment. She had to accept it as her due, but all the same her heart contracted in fear as she thought of the reception she would get when she arrived at her parent's cottage. How there just wouldn't be the room, or the food ... And where would her baby fit among the scrabbling youngsters, most of whom found their way early to the churchyard, their frail bodies unable to cope with the hunger and deprivation which was their lot.

During the next few weeks a deep gloom descended on the household, touching everyone, from Mrs. Thomas who, however much she blamed the back end of the year, knew that she was missing her Harry and the boys, to Twm who felt keenly the loss of a good shepherd. Fortunately the pressure of work was increasing; lambing had begun in earnest and kept the men occupied and their minds from brooding although there was little heart in the evenings for the usual song and story. Even Jencyn, although his faith was vindicated, felt touched by the despondency and he found himself depressed by the thought of Jenette's fate, even though the punishment was God's, and just, and deserved.

Catrin found that her feelings fluctuated between high optimism and deep despair. Sometimes she would awake in the morning with mounting hope that the day would bring news of Simon. That the news would be good; that he was on his way back, or that his cause was in the ascendancy. She would day-dream of his return, of their re-union, of their wedded bliss, of years of fortune and happiness. Then on other occasions the future appeared hopeless, the difficulties insurmountable, Simon's danger catastrophic. On those days, the valley and hillside which had provided such a happy play-ground during her childhood years, confined her like a sinister prison, offering no hope, handing out only despair.

On one of these fearful, apprehensive days, a day of disquiet and misgiving, Catrin decided to seek the aid of Old Meg. She had been once before to the old woman's mud and wattle hut. On that occasion she had begged a potion for her brother, and had been told the magic words to use for fever. They had been spoken too late to save Will, but the incantation had worked with Simon. Catrin remembered now how she had urged Simon to eat the apple portions while she uttered the spell. She recalled the sceptical smile drawn from him despite his ague, and remembered too how he had been made whole again.

Some said Old Meg could see into the future, although few were brave enough to face her with a request. Her cottage lay beyond the church, tucked away in a hollow of the hillside and shrouded by a thick copse. A traveller would have passed by without knowledge of a habitation, but the local people were only too aware of Old Meg's existence. She was regarded with fear, and offerings, perhaps a jug of cream, or a rabbit, or a loaf of bread, were brought to her hut and laid outside as an insurance. Old Meg would know by her Black Arts the identity of the benefactor, and he would be protected for a while from the devastating effects of her Evil Eye. Her knowledge of folk medicine was extensive although mixed with superstition. Incantations were invariably needed for her remedies to work, but she dispensed her potions and ointments to those who had the courage to ask, and begged only a morsel of food in return.

Few people had been inside her small hut. When Catrin had called before, the old woman had been tending her small herb garden and had given her advice ungraciously in exchange for a portion of bread and cheese. Today, Catrin tied a piece of bacon and a loaf in a cloth, and mounting Sheba, guided the horse to the bridge and across the river. Her heart was pounding as she neared the thicket which guarded Old Meg's cottage, and the grey sky and the mist which clung to the shrubs and veiled branch and twig, boded and spoke to Catrin of the stories of sorcery and witchcraft which were passed around among the company in the farm kitchen during the long winter nights. Many people kept talismans against such evil; superstitious relics from the old times, metal crosses or rough-hewn statues, or beads once used for prayer.

Catrin had no such charm and if she had not been desperate to see what lay ahead, to know what fate held in store for herself and for Simon, she would have turned and fled when the hut, a small tumble-down erection needing a fresh wash of white came into view. The door was closed and Catrin hesitated before knocking. The sound of her palm striking the damp wood echoed in the silent close, but no one answered her call. She knocked a second and a third time without effect, then lifting the latch, she collected all her courage and opened the door.

At first she could see nothing in the blackness which greeted her. She put her hand to her face too, for a stench compounded of damp, mildew and stale urine reached her like a gust of foul wind. After a few moments her eyes grew accustomed to the darkness and she saw that in fact a dull glow from the dying embers of a fire shed a little light into the bare room. Another shaft of illumination sprang from a small window which was unglazed, a few wooden slates providing poor protection from the elements. On a rough bed of hay in a corner lay Old Meg, her breath coming in great painful gasps. With effort she sat up when the girl entered and held out two skinny arms.

"What have you brought? Old Meg is starving. No one came. No one."

"Here, *Mamgu*. Some bread and a piece of fat bacon."

The old woman snatched the loaf and tore at it with blackened teeth. Catrin, her fear abated by shocked horror, waited silently while the edge was taken from the old woman's hunger.

"Bless you," Meg croaked. "Put the bacon in the pot. All I've had for days has been turnip."

Catrin took the meat over to the *crochan* which

was suspended over the fire. Inside, a few pieces of vegetable matter floated in greasy water. The girl added the bacon and felt like vomiting. She went outside for more wood and after gulping some fresh air returned to the fetid room to build up the fire.

"You're a good girl."

Catrin looked sharply at the old woman. "They say you are in league with the Devil. Why doesn't he look after you?"

"They say, they say. They say anything but their prayers. I am a Sabbath child. I came into the world three hours after sunrise and I can understand the language of spirits. I have powers." The morsel of food had strengthened Old Meg and her nut-cracker face gained in force. "I know things others do not, but the Devil! Bah!" She spat contemptuously on to the floor. "Curses, or the fear of them bring me food. How else would I eat?"

"They say that you can see into the future?"

"The veil sometimes parts." The old woman relapsed into silence, but her watery eyes stared at Catrin, at the cloud of hair highlighted by a shaft of light from the window, at the soft curve of the girl's cheek. "Why should you want to know? You have life, young life, spirit. Enjoy what you have without fear of the future."

"But things go wrong. Terribly wrong. I must know, *Mamgu*" The girl clasped the woman's hand, pleading, begging. "Someone is in danger. Someone I love ... I brought you bacon. . . ."

The old woman grunted. "You are a fool ... but a kindhearted fool." She took a stick and drew a sign on the earthen floor, muttering as she did so. Then she took a handful of straw and flung it over the symbol. She held Catrin's shawl tightly as she stared at the random pattern on the floor. Fear crept inside Catrin once more as she waited for the woman's words, and when they came they brought desolation.

"Death!" the old woman cried. "I see Death. Death of a loved one."

"Death!" Catrin, white-faced, repeated the dame's words and felt hope and delight drain from her. She had told Simon he was putting his head in a noose. If only he had listened to her!

"Is... is that all you see?" Wasn't it enough? What could mitigate the sentence which had just been passed?

"I see a jewel, deep red, glowing, burning. Your fortune lies within it." The old woman turned her face towards Catrin's and clutched her arm. "Take what it offers you. Don't be afraid." She lay back on her bed, suddenly exhausted. "Go you now, and leave me in peace."

Sheba stood outside the cottage, swathed in the increasing mist. She whinnied as Catrin closed the door behind her and nuzzled the girl when she approached. Catrin buried her head in the horse's mane. "Oh, Sheba, Sheba, what is to become of us all."

Visiting Old Meg had been a mistake. Catrin knew that now for she realised that she had gone there expecting to find reassurance. But Meg had confirmed her worst fears. Death was taking from her all she loved, was taking her future.

The farmhouse was oppressive that evening.

Catrin and her mother sat in the kitchen hoping to gain a little comfort from the presence of the other members of the household, hoping that a story would be told or a song sung. But since Dic's accident, the farm hands had been dispirited, and they realised that much of the lively chat, the jokes, the good humour, had in fact emanated from the tall redhead who was no longer with them.

Jenette, sitting in the corner solemnly knitting, was too, a damper on the company. Few could forget that she was to leave the household at Easter in the hope that her parents would share their roof with her. Already she had stopped working in the buttery, for it would have brought bad luck to the household for a pregnant woman to share the tasks associated with the dairy.

When the door opened and Shoni entered with his harp, closely followed by Griff, Catrin's heart lightened. Perhaps now there would be a song or a joke, a bantering word to lighten the despondence which had descended on the company.

Twm, indeed, stood up eagerly and welcomed the visitors. "There's glad we are to see you, boys," he said with obvious relief. "Miserable people we are at the moment. What about a clog dance from Griff to cheer us all up?"

The two men shuffled in shamefacedly. Shoni left his harp near the door and ambled over to the hearth to warm his hands. Griff cleared his throat as if he had an important message to give, but he looked nervously at his companion and said nothing.

"The fact is," Shoni began. "The truth of the matter is ... that Griff won't be dancing nor I singing, that is, not like I was used to do."

"Shame on you, Shoni." Anne Thomas spoke loud and clear. "Relying on you we were, to cheer everyone up."

"Terrible things have happened."

"Terrible," echoed Griff.

"They were a punishment for our evil ways." Shoni wiped his brow and forced himself to look Twm in the eye.

"It is true," Griff added. "My clogs have I burnt in the fire. Better that, than we should all go to the furnace."

"The preacher came from over the mountain," explained Shoni. "A prayer meeting we had at Richard's Cwm Du. The Lord spoke to us and we listened."

Jencyn emerged from his corner and shook each of the men warmly by the hand. Then he stood straight on the flagstones and lifted his arms high.

"Praise to you, Lord." His mellow voice resounded from the stone walls of the building . "You have shown mercy to your people. Those who stood in darkness have seen great light ...."

Catrin listened bemused as the man's voice rose a semitone with each chanting sentence until ending on a note of high-pitched fervour, a *hwyl* of emotion, it descended to grave normality. The room was charged with feeling as each man dropped his head prayerfully into his hands. Only Catrin and her mother stood straight, resisting the Presence which had come into their midst.

Jencyn finished speaking and silence descended

on the room until Shoni brought his harp from the wall and began to pluck the strings. Only this time it was no happy, bawdy song which roused merriment to be echoed by the rafters. The limpid minor chords evoked repentance, the extempore verse reminded the listeners of the tribulations of the children of Israel, of the necessity to eschew the pleasures of this world if the glory of God was to be revealed.

At the hymn's close, Jenette left her stool and stood in the centre of the floor with bowed head. "I have sinned," she whispered. "Flightly I have been, not hearing the word of God or walking in His ways."

Jencyn drew near and placed his hand on her shoulder. "Look upon your daughter with mercy, Lord," he implored. "Sinful she has been, and her punishment is with her. Help her to turn away from wickedness and to dwell in Thy house."

Jenette sniffed, then from her pocket she drew a handful of bright ribands. Catrin recognised them as those she had given the girl when her forthcoming marriage was announced, and she started with anger as the servant held them over the fire. Jenette slowly let them fall from her fingers and they dropped into the flames, flaring with life before they were reduced to white ash.

"So may all my follies be consumed." The girl quietly resumed her place on her stool and picked up her interminable knitting, the long grey stocking which occupied the moments she was free from housework.

Shoni began another hymn and Catrin rose suddenly and left the kitchen, frightened that she too, might be grasped by the demanding faith which required such sacrifice. She ran to her room and through the window looked up to the stars, which now that the wind had risen to chase away the remnants of fog, were shining clear in a sable sky.

She prayed too ... that Old Meg should be wrong ... that Simon would live . . . would come back to her. And because she was young and the blood pulsed through her veins with longing and desire, and because the years spread before her waiting to be filled with love and with laughter, she drew comfort from the sparkling Heavens. Simon lay under the same sky, dreaming the same dreams. How then could those dreams rest unfulfilled?

EIGHT

A few days later a commotion in the forecourt of the farmhouse caused Catrin and her mother to run to the parlour window. Outside, his large frame protected from the elements by a massive cloak and shoulder cape, a severe tricorne hat firmly wedged on his wig and shadowing the line of his bulbous nose and fleshy cheeks, Griffith Evans clambered heavily from his horse. He was accompanied by a servant who dutifully took the mounts around to the stables.

The women watched while their visitor stood back and looked critically at the frontage of the house. He pursed his lips as he noticed the broken shingles on the eaves and pulled a face at the chipped stone coping which decorated the door frame. A look of revulsion passed over Anne Thomas' face; a sentiment which she quickly suppressed. As the man approached the door, Catrin turned to leave the room but her mother put a restraining hand on her arm.

"Let one of the servants go to the door," she admonished. The Thomases didn't usually stand on ceremony. Life was too hard on the farmsteads, even those with some pretensions to gentility, for much pride, but Griffith Evans must be shown that the Thomas women were not to be accounted too lightly.

So, when Mari showed the visitor into the parlour, Catrin and her mother were sitting near the hearth, occupied with the interminable knitting which was the lot of the women, high or low of the area, their faces composed but wary.

Anne Thomas rose. "Take Mr. Evans' cloak and hat, Mari, and bring him some ale and oatcakes." She turned to the visitor. *"Eisteddwch,* Mr. Evans. I beg your pardon," she corrected herself in English. "Please sit down."

Griffith Evans spluttered and coughed into a large kerchief but lowered himself into the chair offered, looking around the room with a hard, proprietorial air as he did so.

"You've improved this place, Ma'am."

"I like to think so. The *cwpwrdd tridarn* is new. Made only three years ago by Evan Watkins of Llantrisant."

Evans nodded speculatively. The three-piece cupboard was a fine article with good carvings which spoke of the touch of a master craftsman. He would have to see this Evan Watkins himself. The item of course would have been acquired before Harry Evans mortgaged the farm so heavily to him, but he noted its presence with satisfaction as he did the fine set of pewter plates and jugs which stood on its shelves.

"I merely called in to pay my respects, Ma'am. And to enquire how you fared during the bad weather."

"Tolerably, Mr. Evans. We lost very few animals, although we were not as well prepared as we would have been had Harry and Will still been here."

Evans shook his head solemnly. "A bad business, Mrs. Thomas. And it has left you in an unfortunate position. Financially, I mean."

A hot spot appeared in each of Anne Thomas' cheeks and her knitting needles clicked more fiercely.

"Now, I'm not a hard man." The sly, brown eyes looked at Anne astutely. "Nevertheless, I regard my property and any loans I make as a business. The time will come ... the time will come . . ." his voice grew in portentiousness as he spoke, "... for repayment."

"I am well aware of that fact." Anne Thomas' back had straightened and she regarded Mr. Evans' face coldly, noting the large pores on his coarse skin, the silvery bristle on his cheeks, the growing dewlap which touched his cravat. "You will be paid in full. Just give us a little time."

"Do not disturb yourself, Ma'am. We may be able to come to some sort of ... arrangement." He paused. Anne was a fine looking woman although in her late thirties, and he liked the way she hadn't whined when he mentioned the mortgage. He couldn't stand women who wept. "Yes," he added pensively. "Something may be arranged ...."

Anne, aware of the implications of his remarks, stood hurriedly. If Griffith Evans asked her, she would accept as a way out of difficulty, as a means to acquiring the material goods she craved, as an insurance for her daughter who would stand a better chance of a good marriage. But not today. Let him not ask her today. Please God, he would give her time to get used to the idea.

"You will be staying for dinner, Mr. Evans? I must see that chickens are put on the spit."

"Thank you, Mrs. Thomas. While you are seeing to the domestic side, I might have a look over the farm. Inspect the livestock. I understand that you have a good strain of dairy cows."

"One of the men will take you."

"I'll see if I can find Twm." Catrin left her seat by the fire, glad to escape from the unease she always felt in Griffith Evans' presence.

"Don't trouble yourself." Evans caught her arm as she made for the door and held her hand a little too long, a shade too sensuously. His eyes glinted as he felt his pulse rate rise. This was the filly he wanted most of all. He must not act rashly. Undoubtedly Anne Thomas would make a good wife, the rounded curves of her breasts promised a warmth of delight in his bed, but the girl ... Catrin's virginity, her freshness, called to him, made him feel a young man, made him forget his growing paunch, his greying hair, his loose teeth. There may be a way . . . Griffith Evans had learned through many years of sharp practice and hard bargaining, that most of the people with whom he wrangled had some sort of Achilles heel, a secret of some kind hidden among their family affairs. The Thomases were probably no different from their fellows. If he could find a weak spot ... He already held them in a firm grip. No harm to try to tighten his hold further.

"I'll find someone myself," he added as Catrin side-stepped away from him. "That fellow you brought to Ynysbedw. Jencyn ... Jencyn something or other,"

"Jencyn ap Dafydd," Anne supplied.

"That's right. He'll do."

Jencyn was in the kitchen when the women

118

entered to hustle the maids and supervise the extra cooking, and Anne unsuspectingly sent him to escort Griffith Evans.

"He wants to see around the farm, Jencyn," she told the man. "Show the best now, the new lambs in Maes Glas and the black cattle which will go to market next month."

Griffith Evans was waiting in the farmyard, hens scrabbling around his feet and a goose in the goose-box by the kitchen door honking at his intrusion, not recognising his thick figure and heavy wig. The servant approached warily, remembering the coin he had been given at Ynysbedw, his assignment to provide information. To his immediate relief, Evans mentioned neither.

"The stable first, Jencyn," he announced. "Let's see what you've got here in the way of good nags."

The morning was fine, the sun warming stone and path and showering encouragement over the swelling buds on the bare branches of the trees and on the first of the spring flowers which were bravely beginning to emerge. Griffith took his time, inspecting minutely the outbuildings and barns, the implements, the looms in the weaving shed, the bakery warm with the sweet smell of new bread. He was impressed with the quality of the herds grazing on the hillside and did not fail to note Jencyn's ability to analyse, to predict results, or that his ideas on organisation and husbandry were sound. Their furthest point of inspection was the old barn where Simon had spent a comfortless night.

"This place hasn't been used for some time," Jencyn remarked. "With a little attention it could be brought into use if we increased cultivation in the top meadow."

Evans was only giving him half his attention. A pile of hay, indented as if it had been used as a bed had caught his astute gaze. A hunk of hard bread and a piece of cheese, blue with mould, were half hidden by a bundle of straw.

"You said that no one had been here." Evans pointed to the hay. "I would say that you have had a visitor."

"A visitor, we have had," remarked Jencyn smoothly, "but not in the barn."

"Come you must tell me about this." Griffith Evans left the barn and strolled back towards the house.

"Remembering I am our agreement." Jencyn's face was a close study as he looked blandly at Evans.

"Of course, of course, man. I haven't forgotten. Why do you think I came? Your reward will depend on what you tell me."

There was much to tell. The visit of the map-maker recorded in detail, an account of Catrin's wanderings at dawn on Sheba. Their sudden cessation, which Jencyn had not failed to notice, and which may or may not have been due to the inclement weather.

By the time they had reached the farmhouse, now rich with the smell of roasting meat, Griffith Evans' face bore signs of smug satisfaction. He pressed a coin into Jencyn's hand.

"Good man. Keep your eyes open."

His spirits were high during the meal which was served in style in the now little-used dining room. His eyes rested often on Catrin, on her neat figure, on the hair falling in a glossy lock over her smooth neckline, on her sombre dark eyes, on her red, curving lips. With luck, the farm and the girl would be his!

Although few would have believed it possible, Jencyn's thoughts were taking a parallel path. He sat at the kitchen table supping at a bowl of broth and although he said little to further the conversation among the farm hands he threw a surreptitious glance now and then at Jenette. The girl sat opposite him, her eyes downcast, eating without enthusiam. Although her young, healthy body with its growing burden called out for food, she was too dispirited to enjoy it. Jencyn looked with approval at the plain cap which covered the girl's hair, and at the kerchief tucked inside her bodice, completely masking the generous curves which lay beneath.

Since the night of the impromptu prayer meeting, the night Jenette had accused herself of her sin, Jencyn had wrestled within himself. At first he had thought it was the Devil which still roused him to dreams of lust over the girl. He spent sleepless nights trying to control his mounting passion, but even calling on God's help ceased to soothe him. Eventually he began to wonder if his prayer for mercy for the girl had been heard and gradually an idea emerged, at first unthinkable, later becoming feasible and then desirable.

That afternoon, when Mr. Evans and his servant had taken their leave, Jencyn sought out Mrs. Thomas.

She looked at him suspiciously as he entered the parlour. "What do you want, Jencyn?" Experience had taught her that the man weighed each word carefully and usually to his own advantage.

"I should like to speak about Jenette, Mistress."

"Jenette? What of her? The girl is suffering enough if you have come to suggest more penance."

"Not at all. I should like to marry her."

Ann Thomas dropped her knitting and Catrin who had been gazing out of the window turned sharply to face the servant.

"She has repented of her sin. The cottage is ready for us. I am prepared to take on the responsibilities of marriage."

"I am beginning to understand. Go and find Jenette, Catrin."

The servant girl entered the room hesitantly. She looked fearfully at Jencyn before addressing herself defensively to Mrs. Thomas.

"You said I could stay until Easter, Mistress."

"No one is sending you away. Prepare for a shock, Jenette. This man wishes to marry you."

"I can't believe it!" The girl swayed and Catrin guided her to a chair.

Jencyn managed a tense smile. "You have repented Jenette, and God is merciful. With Mrs. Thomas' permission, we can live in the cottage."

"But that was to have been mine and Dic's ..."

The distress showed plainly on the girl's face and Jencyn winced at this reminder.

"And now it will be yours and Jencyn's," replied Anne Thomas with resolution. Although she did not envy Jenette's life with Jencyn, the girl had no choice.

"At Halloween ... my apple peel ... it fell into a

122

D. How then am I to marry Jencyn?"

"But Jencyn has a 'D' too." Catrin reminded her. "Jencyn ap Dafydd."

Jenette nodded limply, convinced by superstition of a fate she knew she should welcome. "I will be a good wife, Jencyn," she whispered.

"You can marry next week," said Mrs. Thomas firmly. "That will give us time to send out the Bidder again. You are going to need his efforts."

Despite brave attempts at jollity it was a sober enough wedding. Even the 'bride-hunt' was half-hearted, the party seeking to hide the bride being only too ready for her to be captured and brought to the church. Perhaps the shade of Dic hung too sharply over the proceedings, but even so, people gave generously to the Bidding and Jenette and Jencyn were able to furnish their small one-room cottage with the semblance of comfort. Mrs. Thomas baked a large cake and while it was being cut Catrin escaped to the solitude of her room.

The ceremony, strained though it was with tension, had moved her strangely. She had listened to the vows the couple exchanged in a torment of spirit. Would she and Simon ever make those promises? Would she ever stand by his side and pledge her life to his? Old Meg's prophecy layover her like a pall, yet she refused to believe that she would never see Simon again. Hope, wishful thinking, call it what you will, sustained her, promised that one day all would be well.

Now, reaching the haven of her room, Catrin opened the lid of her oak chest. From beneath the pile of clothes she lifted Simon's embroidered coat. The sunlight shafting through the window, lit on its rich colours, glinted on the gold braid which trimmed pockets and button-holes. She ran her hand over the encrusted fabric, remembering Simon, their encounter at the old well, his frank blue eyes, his smile, merry and yet tender. She shuddered to think of his fate if he fell into the hands of his enemies. He had had no illusions himself about what would happen to him, and yet he had plunged into danger. Catrin picked up the sword and as she held its gleaming scabbard, she breathed a prayer that he would keep safe and return to her. She was afraid to daydream further than that. The future was clouded with such difficulties. All Catrin could cling to was the hope that Old Meg was wrong and that Death was not in ambush for her loved one.

She started in alarm as Jenette ran into the room.

"Mistress Catrin!" The girl halted, surprised. "I didn't know ... I only came for a jug I left here ..."

Her voice petered out as her gaze fell on the shining sword in Catrin's hands. A prism of colour beamed from its decorated hilt, dazzling Jenette with its brilliance. She noticed the coat, the rich cloth hinting of luxury never enjoyed by anyone of her acquaintance.

"Tell no one, Jenette." Catrin rose and there was an anxious urgency in her tone. "Promise me that this will be a secret between us."

The girl looked bewildered and Catrin realised that she would not understand the significance of the sword and coat. Perhaps she was unwise to stress the secrecy, yet what else could she do?

"I'll say nothing, Mistress Catrin," Jenette

promised. "Who should I tell?"

Jencyn, thought Catrin bitterly, *now that you are married to him.* She drew a little comfort by reminding herself that the girl would not yet be used to confiding in the man.

The servant collected the jug and returned to the farm kitchen where the well-wishers were beginning to take leave of Mrs. Thomas before returning to the hamlet across the river. With a pang Jenette thought how different it would all have been if her bridegroom had been Dic. Then the ale would have flowed and the gathering would have been loud in merriment. She resolutely pushed the thought from her. She had put aside that way of life forever and although the thought of bedding with Jencyn made her recoil with distaste, she was wise enough to feel relief that her future was assured, and to feel gratitude also towards the man who had rescued her.

"Come, Jenette," he said now. "A fire there is, burning brightly in our own hearth. We will bid adieu to the company and make our way ... home!"

A feeling of great satisfaction swept through him as he drew Jenette's arm through his and led her through the fields to their cottage. God had been good to him, but it was because he had listened to His word and done His bidding. He had prayed for a wife and a place of his own but he wasn't done yet. A cottage would do for the time being but Jencyn had further ambitions. He knew that he would not be satisfied until a place like Ty Celyn was in his hands.

The kitchen denuded of company, Mrs. Thomas retired to the parlour. For some hours her old pain had been niggling at her, beginning as usual with cramps across her stomach which made her want to double up for ease. Now they had grown worse and had developed into sharp stabs in her right side. When Catrin entered the room she found her mother grey-faced with pain, leaning for support across the back of a chair. Alarmed, Catrin helped her to a seat by the fire.

"What can I bring?" she asked anxiously. Although she knew her mother had been troubled from time to time with colic, she had never before seen the woman in such a state.

"You could make me a decoction of groundsel," she suggested. "It is recommended for colicky pains and was beneficial when I administered it to Mari last year."

Catrin nodded. Her mother had a fund of knowledge concerning herbs and in the *cwpwrdd triban* kept jars of neatly labelled dried leaves and roots. The girl now took groundsel into the kitchen and returned after a while with a cup of steaming liquid. Her mother forced herself to drink the mixture and then stood, bent, leaning on her daughter.

"You'll have to help me to bed," she said. "For to walk properly is impossible for me."

Catrin felt a pang of fear as she put her arm around her mother's waist and gently guided her up the stairs and into her room. Although it was growing dusk, there were still duties to be attended to in the house and kitchen, and Catrin had never before known her mother to retire to bed before all the chores had been completed. The pain must be very intense, she realised, to make Anne Thomas take to her bed.

"You could bring me a poultice," she considered

as Catrin drew the quilt around her shoulders. "Make it with hot camomile flowers, for it has wonderful comfort for torments of the belly."

Her breath was coming in short gasps as she fought the increasing pain. When Catrin placed the hot poultice over her stomach, her mother gave her a weak smile and clasped her hand gratefully.

That night, Catrin slept beside her mother in the big bed and was relieved to find that after a few hours Anne Thomas dropped off into a fitful sleep. Catrin herself slept then, deeply and dreamlessly, as if her body was providing an insulation against worry and dread. She was awakened in the dawn by the sound of her mother retching over the side of the bed into a bowl.

"The pain is back," she gasped as she lay back exhausted against the pillows. Her cheeks were hollow and bloodless and Catrin was alarmed at the way her mother had seemingly aged in a few short hours.

"I shall send Jencyn to Llantrisant for the doctor," Catrin told her mother but the woman shook her head.

"What good will he do? What did he do for poor Harry or Will or Evan? He just filled their last hours with more anguish from the blisters he put on their sores." She reached out for Catrin's hand and pressed it reassuringly. "I'll be better soon. You'll see. Although I haven't been as bad as this before, the pains have often been with me. And always they have passed."

Nevertheless, in spite of her determination to get well, Anne Thomas was unable to rise from her bed that day and when night fell, and Catrin joined her again, her moans increased and she began to shiver with the ague. Catrin put a wrapper over her shift and brought candles to the side of the bed. She looked down on her mother suffering so helplessly and cradling the woman's head in her arms prayed fiercely for her recovery.

"God grant that I may not lose another loved one," she whispered, and as the words left her lips she froze with the memory of Old Meg's prophecy. *"Death,"* the woman had croaked, *"death, of a loved one."*

Catrin had thought only of Simon, already in danger, but it was of her mother that the old crone had spoken!

As if she had followed the trend of the girl's thoughts, Anne Thomas opened her eyes and gazed at her daughter. "It is all over for me, Catrin," she said. "Three days ago, I was in the fields at dusk and the *cannwyll gorff,* the corpse candles, appeared to me. Hovering over the hedges they were, white lights changing to red and blue as they moved towards me, and the air as quiet as Death. I ran indoors and pretended that nothing had happened, that the lights were a reflection from the shining moon. I didn't want to die, Catrin. In spite of all that has happened to us, all our difficulties and our sorrows, I wanted to live. Now I know that my fate is sealed."

"Don't say such things, mother. You are mistaken. You will get well."

"Don't distress yourself, Catrin. We cannot fight what has to be. But there is something I must do before I leave you."

The woman's brow was sweating with effort and

Catrin moistened a cloth and drew it over her mother's face and forehead.

"Open my chest, Catrin. Right at the bottom you will find a wooden box. Bring it to me."

Catrin lifted the heavy lid and rummaged underneath her mother's clothes and the pile of linen kept inside. She lifted out a small oak casket blackened with age, and handed it to her mother.

"There is a key in my pocket, Catrin."

Catrin fetched it and her mother turned it in the lock and lifted the hinged lid.

"This has been in the Thomas family for generations," she told the girl, "but only one person at a time knows of its existence. Your father entrusted it to me before he died, as I am doing to you. See what is inside."

Catrin lifted out a carving, rough hewn from oak. It was a representation of a woman, standing on a cushion of oak leaves and holding a child. On the mother's head was a crown.

"Once there was a similar statue, high on Penrhys," Anne Thomas went on. "That was made of oak too, and some say that it was miraculous, having appeared overnight, and that no one could move it until a chapel had been built. But see what else lies there."

Catrin drew out a long necklace made of glistening gold and encrusted with sparkling rubies. She gasped as they caught fire in the light of the candles and flashed crimson beams across her fingers.

"The statue was hung with jewels, left there by countless, grateful pilgrims." Anne Thomas took up

129

her tale although pain still racked her body and the fever was beginning to steal her wits. "The King, Henry Tudor, took them when the statue was carted off to Smithfield to be burnt, but one of the Thomases found the necklet hidden in the bushes soon after. It has stayed in the family ever since and no one has sold it, although money has been short and difficulties have been many. One day it is said, it will save the family, but the Lady will tell us when. It belongs to her. *Mair 0 Benrhys.*"

"Mary of Penrhys!" echoed Catrin.

"Keep it safely," gasped the dying woman. "One day it will be needed."

The trinket slid through Catrin's fingers to its resting place in the casket. As the girl locked it once more, her mother sank deeper into the pillows, her breath caught in painful rasps. Catrin caught hold of the woman's hands, willing her to recover, but she knew it was too late. Anne's fingers, once so active, so busy with churning, with baking, so clever with healing concoctions, so soothing in love, were stilled forever.

Catrin dropped a kiss on the lifeless forehead and silently left the room.

NINE

If Dic's sudden death had sobered the small community, Anne's going confirmed its gloom and reinforced the guilt which hung over the valley. Until the funeral, the dead woman lay in the parlour, the many mourners, from up the valley and down, calling into the room to pay their respects and then retiring to the kitchen for hot ale. Once again the conviviality of the normal wake was missing. The bereft figure of Catrin, tight-lipped, her cheeks unusually hollowed, her eyes refusing tears although these may have washed away some of the sorrow, reminded visitors and servants alike that this was the third loss that the girl had suffered in the course of one year. In dark corners talk turned to speculation on curses. Some believed that a deep purpose was unfolding, others that malevolent spirits must hold Ty Celyn in thrall. Faces became shadowed with dread even though Jencyn pointed out that no one need fear evil if he put his trust in God. Many eyes were turned anxiously towards the copse where Old Meg lived in squalor, and the offerings left outside her hovel increased for a while in frequency.

The funeral service itself was attended by all the farmers of importance in the parish. The Thomas family, even when hard pressed by trials of finance and allegiance, had exerted much influence for generations in the small community. Now its sole representative was one young girl. Eyes were turned speculatively towards her as her slight, lonely figure followed the oak casket. What would she make of her fortune? The word was a misnomer. There was little enough left of her patrimony to support her if gossip was well founded.

One mourner who had more knowledge than most about the state of Catrin's inheritance, was Griffiths Evans. He stood by the graveside as the clods of earth struck hollowly on the coffin, and his eyes strayed to Catrin. The sombre band swathing her tricorne hat emphasised by sheer contrast her youthful freshness, and Evans felt a twist of desire. Anne's death had shocked him more than he cared to admit. The news had reached him while he was sitting smoking near the hearth, and turning over in his mind the advantages and disadvantages of a marriage with Anne. For a while he had been too stunned to make other plans, although the implications of the situation had not escaped him. Now Anne was safely put away. Death had been too frequent a visitor during Griffith Evans' life for him to waste any time in fruitless regrets. Like his two wives and his dead children, Anne would soon become a past memory. He was alive; his blood coursed through his veins as fiercely as ever; for him there was a future. A future which would bring him not only the potential of Ty Celyn, a farm which in his opinion had never been exploited to its fullest extent, but would deliver to his arms a young and beautiful bride.

So he was in good spirits when back at the farmhouse he mingled with the other mourners. Many of them had travelled for miles to attend the funeral, and needed to sustain themselves with the boiled bacon, the broth, the oatcakes and the ale which Catrin had provided. The labourers and the small farmers entertained themselves in the kitchen, but those with pretensions to gentility settled in the parlour where Catrin poured fruit wine for the wives. Griffith Evans was among these guests and he made a point of standing near Catrin. If she eased away under the pretext of her duties of hostess, it was not long before she found that he was once more at her elbow.

"Don't forget, my dear Mistress Thomas," he told her, and the new title startled Catrin, brought her poignantly to face the fact that she was indeed now mistress of the household, "don't forget, that if you need any advice, or indeed help, you have only to ask. No doubt things will be difficult for you for quite a while."

"I'm sure I shall manage. My thanks all the same. You are most kind." Catrin's voice wavered only slightly. Her last phrase was, she knew, insincere. Evans was motivated by anything but kindness but she had to tread carefully. She knew that he held a mortgage on the farm although the extent of the debt had never been disclosed to her. Nevertheless she was sure that a few years good management of the farm would be sufficient to repay all she owed.

"There will be problems." Evans' voice was blunderingly insistent. "Managing a farm like this is a man's job."

"Simon's job," thought Catrin, *"if only he could be here".*

Aloud she said, "The men are good, reliable ... Twm knows the farm like the back of his hand, and there is our new hand, Jencyn." Catrin pushed aside her dislike of the man. He was something of a scholar and she was going to need all the help she could find.

"Yes. Jencyn. A clever fellow." Evans nodded. He wanted a word with Jencyn himself before he left. He lifted Catrin's hand to his lips to take his leave and the girl suppressed a shudder of distaste. "I shall be over one day when you have had time to settle down. We have to talk business. As you probably know, I have more than a small interest in Ty Celyn and this might lead you into difficulties. But," he held Catrin's slim fingers between his own fleshy hands, "there is always a way to solve difficulties. And I can think of an admirable way to solve this one."

His eyes met Catrin's as he spoke, raking her sensuously, his dewlap quivering in anticipation of possessing his prize. She evaded the arm which was about to encircle her shoulder in a mock paternal gesture, and dipping in a slight curtsey began to attend to her other guests. Her hands trembled as she poured drinks and she felt alarm overlie the grief which had swamped her for the past few days. Remembering her previous conversation with her mother, she had no doubt that Griffith Evans was going to propose marriage. She also felt that hard stubborn streak of independence, which had characterised her family from time immemorial, rise within her. Even had she not met Simon, there would have been little doubt as to her answer. But Simon had come into her life and now even if Evans had been young and personable, he could only expect short shrift from her. Perhaps she did owe money to the man, but there must be, would be, some other way of paying the debt. Selling herself, her body, her soul, her hopes, her longings, her future, was out; this was something which could never be considered.

Catrin said goodbye to the visitors who were beginning to trickle away in order to reach their homes before sunset, and then walked alone through the house. The servants, still subdued, were in the kitchen or yard, and Catrin standing alone felt the walls and rafters, silent save for a creaking joint here and there, enclose her. The empty rooms, a few months previously ringing with voices and laughter, were now peopled with ghosts. Catrin drew her shawl closely around her shoulders and shivered. Death was indiscriminate. It struck ruthlessly and unexpectedly, with seemingly no thought of the consequences. She wondered about her own escape. She had never in her life contracted smallpox, that dread disease which had so cruelly taken her father and brothers. During her consultation with Old Meg at the time of their illness the old crone told her that she had not succumbed because when she was a small girl her father, in order that she should learn the art of looking after a farm-stead had insisted that each day she should milk the cows with the dairy-maid. She remembered now, crying, because her hands were sore and blistered. "Cow's magic," an old farm hand had said at the time and the child had wondered fearfully how a cow could cast a spell, and why, and what might be the outcome.

She wandered around the empty house, touching the *cwpwrdd triban* with its sensitive carvings and remembering the pride her mother had shown when it was brought into the house. She fingered her father's tobacco bowl, Evan's books, the love-spoon Will had been carving for his sweetheart when he had been struck down. No one was left but her and Simon. Simon must not die! He would not die! Catrin willed it so, fiercely, angrily. They were survivors, she and Simon. Their place was together.

To Catrin's relief many weeks passed with no word from Griffith Evans. They were busy weeks. Easter came and went and the work on the farm was exacting. Twm was no longer the prop that Anne Thomas had believed him to be. The winter had taken its toll, aged him, left him depressed with little to cheer him. Even so, Catrin realised that he was not a decision maker. He had served the family well for many years but always under the expert direction of her father. Catrin had no option but to watch Jencyn take over the reins of management. The man was efficient and hard-working; she could find no fault with his behaviour and yet she still disliked and mistrusted him. She rarely sat in the kitchen in the evenings, glad that the lengthening days prolonged the hours when work was possible. Merry songs were a thing of the past, even now that Jencyn had his own cottage and his own hearth. He held a prayer meeting at Ty Celyn twice a week, and once a visiting preacher called.

The curate protested to Catrin about this defection in his flock. "You should not allow it, Mistress Thomas. They have a church to go to. That is the place for their prayers."

"There is little enough comfort in life, Mr. Howell," Catrin replied, her eyes sombre and reflecting. "Perhaps it helps them. Their work has improved. They are taking their duties more seriously since Jencyn has taken them over."

The curate pursed his lips. "What is the church for if not to give spiritual comfort?"

"Why then is it falling down?" Catrin regretted the sharp words once they had passed her lips. Mr. Howell was not responsible for the broken windows and the torn roof. His stipend was barely enough to feed his family and he was only able to keep his own roof repaired by tutoring the children of nearby farmers. Catrin herself had learnt her letters at his knee.

Although her response might have been different at some other time, she was now too dispirited to take up issue with Jencyn. Sometimes, during the long, warm evenings, she took Sheba out to ride on the hills. She found solace in the soft, springy turf of the summits, and invariably her gaze turned eastwards. Somewhere out there, over the valley and the hills, was a plain which led eventually to London and Simon. Catrin, remembering his clear-cut features, his eyes, blue and searching, the gentle quirk of his lips, longed for his return. Each morning she prayed for news that day - for good news.

Her nights were filled with dreams. One dream she was always able to recall, and in this dream she was walking through an endless forest of oak trees. The gnarled trunks rose high on each side of her, the branches weaving a twisted ceiling over her head. She was searching, although for what she did not know. Sometimes the branches were spotted with bud, sometimes they were covered with green serrated leaves. When Catrin looked up and saw golden acorns clustered on the twigs above she knew that she was drawing near her goal. The next time she dreamed, acorns began to shower over her and she put up her hand to protect herself. When they ceased raining on her head she looked down and saw the brown husks of the seeds change colour and glisten and shine with the hard brilliance of jewels. Crimson beams flashed at her from the rubies which now carpeted the earth and Catrin stooped and picked up a handful. As they ran through her fingers she felt them alter their shape, become flat and round and she watched as their rich, blood red transmuted to the glitter of gold as coins spilled over her palms. Around her the oak trees were burning and in the midst of the hungry flames she could see a wooden figure; the representation of a mother and her child.

Catrin awoke, startled. Dawn was breaking, and through the window the girl could see the sky, washed with the pale glory of the rising sun. The dream had disturbed her; could this be the message for which generations of Thomases had waited? She unlocked the box her mother had given to her and lifted out the necklace. As the dark jewels touched her fingers, she saw again the ruby acorns and remembered their transformation into coin. Old Meg's words came back to her too. *"Your fortune lies within a jewel. Take what it offers you."*

Catrin felt troubled. If she were to sell the rubies how would she go about it? She had no knowledge of values and there would certainly be no one at Llantrisant market who could help her. If she had been given a direction, the opportunity to buy off her debts, why? Her family had been in grave financial trouble before and had not resorted to selling the necklace.

The girl shrugged the matter away for it was time

to rise and attend to the various household tasks. Many times during the last months Catrin had been grateful for the pressure of work, for the never-ending problems brought her by the men and the girls in the dairy. She had little time to brood and that was true of this morning, for as soon as she set foot in the kitchen, there was trouble. One cow gave no milk, three hens should be set, the cream had curdled. The hours flew and Catrin had no time to consider her personal difficulties. Near noon, she was tidying the contents of the cupboard in the parlour when Mari entered the room.

"A man there is at the door," she told her mistress. "A drover. Asking to see you he is."

Catrin stood straight, her heart beating fast, her cheeks suddenly flushed. "Send him in, Mari." She tried to sound composed but her hands were trembling. The drovers who called at the farm now did their initial business with Jencyn. She was content to leave any arrangements for selling cattle to him, only seeing the two men when they needed her signature to any agreement. If a drover was asking for her personally, it could mean only one thing! News of Simon!

"Good-morning, Ma'am." Mari had shown the man in and he stood by the door twirling his wide-brimmed hat around in his hand. "I'm Mr. Wilson, Ma'am. I have a letter for you, Ma'am."

"A letter?"

"You are Mistress Catrin Thomas?"

"That's right."

"I had strict instructions to give you the letter personally, Ma'am. A gentleman in the yard said as

139

how he would take it, but I said that wouldn't do at all. Not at all, Ma'am." The drover pulled a letter from his pocket and handed it over with a flourish.

The flimsy paper burned into Catrin's fingertips as she took it from the stranger. She broke the seal and saw Simon's signature at the foot of a page of closely written script.

"Can I reply?"

"Not unless there is an address. The gentleman told me he didn't rightly know where he would be."

There was no address and the drover was taking his leave when Catrin called him back.

"Can I trust you?"

"If I says 'yes', how are you to know that I am telling the truth? And if I says, 'no', that means that I am an honest dishonest man. I brought you the letter, Ma'am, what more can I say?"

"Are you going to a town where you could sell a valuable necklace for me?"

"Bristol, Ma'am. I shall be there next week. There are rich merchants in Bristol who will pay fortunes for trinkets for their ladies."

"Wait there."

Catrin ran upstairs and only hesitated for a moment when she picked up the necklace. The dream had been an omen. She didn't know why she had to sell the jewels, but sell she must. If she didn't take courage and trust the man downstairs she would be denying her fate.

He gave a low whistle when Catrin handed over the shining bauble. "Now this, Ma'am, is what I calls a fine piece of work. I knows what I'm talking about because I do a lot of this exchanging, buying and selling, barter, or what you will. This will fetch a bit. A good bit. Leave it to me, Ma'am. I'll be back this way in about a month and you will have the money then."

Catrin stifled any misgivings as he left. She had answered what she felt to be the message of her dream. It had taken courage, but Old Meg had said that she should not be afraid.

She took Simon's letter across to the open window, where a soft breeze fanned her face and a shaft of sunlight made reading easier. News was bad, he told her, and although he did not say so directly, for the danger of his letter falling into the wrong hands was great, Catrin judged that his cause was lost. His future was in shreds and there would be no option but for him to go abroad.

"At the present time," Catrin read, "I cannot take you with me, my dearest Kate, but you will always be in my thoughts. One day when fortune favours us we will be together as man and wife. God bless you for coming into my life ... for all that you have done for me...."

Simon promised that before he left for the Continent, he would somehow visit her.

". . . for how can I leave without touching once again your soft skin and hearing again your sweet voice."

Catrin's eyes were wet as she folded the paper and pushed it into the pocket she wore at her waist. But even she could not realise the anguish that had filled Simon as he scratched the words on to the parchment. There was so much that he could not, dare not say in a letter, on account of the danger involved, but also because there were many things which could only be put into spoken words. If he was with Catrin, he could tell her of the desolation he had felt when he had stood on a cold February morning on Tower Hill and watched the execution of the Earl of Derwentwater. He remembered the young Earl from the campaign in the North, as a nobleman with the highest ideals and the most courteous manner. Now he watched him walk with dignity to the black-draped scaffold, receive absolution from his confessor, and die, calling on the name of Jesus. The murmur of the crowd as his head was severed from his body had risen like a great sigh to heaven.

Simon had disappeared among the milling throng to seek the company of other men in hiding. Those who had been captured waited for sentence, for hanging or transportation according to rank or involvement. Those who remained free scuttled like rats in a sewer, stripped of rank and fortune, scheming vainly plots which they knew to be useless, begging sustenance from sympathisers who now would never be counted and who did not wish to know where the men were hiding. News filtered through of the disastrous campaign in Scotland where James had landed in December. Simon learned that the King's progress had been brief, the countryside bleak and snow-bound, the support he had hoped for demoralised. He had sailed back to France in February, his bid for monarchy a failed dream. One by one his wanted supporters were escaping from the country to join him at Avignon.

Simon had no wish to do this. It meant, he knew,

a life of frustrating poverty, unless he decided to serve in one of the armies which were always on the march in Europe and looking for combatants. There was a little money his father had deposited with a trusted friend in London for an emergency, and this could be collected, but it would not serve for long. As he wrote the letter to Catrin he could see no choice other than to earn his living as a soldier and hope that one day his fortunes would change, yet illogically, Simon felt that must be some other way. So day by day he delayed his departure even though staying in London was tantamount to dicing with death.

The letter both comforted and tormented Catrin. Comforted, because the strong, black pen strokes had brought Simon nearer to her, reassured her of his love, his commitment. Tormented, because she was reminded of his great danger and could sense the anguish and disappointments which lay behind the carefully construed sentences. But the missive also brought Catrin confidence, so that when Griffith Evans paid his promised visit to Ty Celyn she was able to meet him with cold determination.

Evans entered the farm through the yard where he dismounted and called a stable-boy to take his horse.

"Is Jencyn here?" He looked around sharply as he spoke and was gratified to see Jencyn, alerted by the tones of a stranger, leave the cowshed and approach him.

"Well?"

"News only of a drover who called with a letter for the mistress."

"A letter." Evans' eyes narrowed shrewdly.

Letters were rare commodities, sent only in times of stress or disaster. "Where did this letter come from?"

"Very silent was the drover. No information could I draw from him." Jencyn noticed the dark dissatisfaction which spread over the other man's face. He added smugly. "Made enquiries I did, at Llantrisant when I was over to the market."

"And?"

"The drover has gone now with a herd of cattle to Somerset. Sailing he is today or tomorrow from Swanbridge to land at Uphill."

"I don't care where he has gone. Where did he come from?" Evans' voice rose in exasperation.

"They do say, from Smithfield."

"From London!" Evans pursed his lips reflectively. What interest had Catrin in London? He gave Jencyn a coin. "Keep your eyes open."

He strode into the farm kitchen where Mari, busy at the *crochan,* looked up in surprise. She would have expected Mr. Evans to knock formally at the front door, but here he was, throwing his cloak over the settle, looking around with a proprietorial air.

"Take me to your mistress."

Mari bobbed a curtsey and led the man into the hall and knocked on the parlour door.

"What is it, Mari?" Catrin began as the girl opened the door, but Evans pushed by and sat heavily in the chair at the head of the table.

Catrin, who had been sitting in the window-seat sewing, rose and approached him frigidly. "You don't stand on ceremony, Mr. Evans."

"I have no need to."

Catrin flinched and turned away from the man's lecherous gaze.

"Sit down, Mistress Thomas. I have business to discuss."

There was a complacency in his tone which alarmed Catrin and she sat at the table as Griffith Evans drew a sheaf of papers from the voluminous pocket in the skirts of his coat.

"You will know that I hold a mortgage on this property." Evans paused as Catrin nodded. "I am sure that you do not know the extent of your debt."

He pushed the papers towards her and she began to read. Her cheeks whitened as she did so and watching her, Evans' lips curved with satisfaction.

"As you see, you owe £300. I have taken the trouble to make an inventory of your stock and effects. In all they would raise £250. So, my dear young woman, if I choose to foreclose you would be in a sorry position."

Catrin rose and faced him challengingly. She was determined to hide the dismay which taughtened her muscles with alarm. "You will be paid, Mr. Evans. Just give me time."

"Time? For a debt like this? How can you expect, as a woman, to run this farm at a profit?"

"I shall do so. I have good hands. Jencyn ...."

"Jencyn will make a good tenant. I shall install him as soon as we are married." He rose, arms outstretched, a salacious smile playing triumphantly on his face. "Don't you see? This is the answer to all your problems."

Catrin stood, her eyes flashing as she backed

from him, her lips drawn into a tight line.

"I shall not marry you, Mr. Evans." she retorted. "I shall be able to pay you in full in a few months' time." She clenched her fists as she spoke. She had little hope that the necklace would fetch £300, but that it would repay a good part of the debt was certain. She would sell some stock to cover the deficit. Meantime she had to play for time.

Evans dropped his arms in surprise. He remembered Jencyn's information about the letter from London and his eyes narrowed shrewdly. The girl stood before him, her body taut, her cheeks flushed with anger, her dark curls tumbling on her neck in random confusion. His heart beat fiercely as his desire for the young girl grew. Her vulnerability coupled with her fierce spirit taunted him. His determination hardened. He would not be thwarted of this prize.

"In that case, we shall wait and see." He turned on his heel and left the room, his flushed face darker than usual. When he reached the yard, he stamped around angrily while Jencyn brought his horse.

"If you want to better yourself, earn yourself a farm, you'll bring me more information. Ride over with it. Don't wait for me to call. Understood, Davies?"

Jencyn watched the man ride furiously through the gate scattering the hens as he passed. The Anglicisation of his name, *ap Dafydd,* "son of David", had startled him, but the implication was not lost. His ambition grew as he stood in the yard and looked at the farm with its stone walls and tiled roof. God moved mysteriously, but there was no doubt in

Jencyn's mind that He rewarded faithful servants. He served God well, so why should he not one day be Mr. Davies of Ty Celyn?

TEN

The next few weeks were anxious ones not only for Catrin but also for the small community in the valley. The horses belonging to Hopkin, Coed Glas, developed the staggers and Rees Morgan's cows dried up and gave no milk. The barn on one of the smaller hill farms burnt down with the loss of some livestock and many farm implements, and the pigs belonging to widowed Mary Jones died from a mysterious disease. Jencyn held a prayer meeting in the farm kitchen to ask deliverance from all these scourges and most of the men from the locality attended.

Shoni arrived with his harp and accompanied by Griff, but both men were belligerent.

"We have given up our evil ways," Shoni protested. "No longer do we profane the Sabbath by playing games in the churchyard. No longer do we drink to excess or give in to lechery. Why then is God punishing us?"

"The truth he is telling," added Griff and he looked challengingly at Jencyn. "The Thomases have been scourged until all that is left of their family is one young girl, and nowhere can you go in the village without stories of loss or trouble."

"We must pray ..." began Jencyn.

"Too long have we been praying and getting no results."

Morris ap Evan the local miller was well known for his hard bargains and his lack of mercy. His mouth twisted cruelly as he spoke. "If evil there is in our midst, then we must tear it away and destroy it."

"Every week I take a pat of butter to Old Meg, but no good has it done me." The speaker was Dafydd ap Harry, the penurious farmer who had lost his barn and who would consequently have difficulty in finding his rent and feeding his family.

"We could do without Old Meg." Morris ap Evan looked around the company as he spoke. "Who will come with me tomorrow? Who will face the Devil's instrument in her own den?"

There was a pause. Most of the men in the room had been brought up in fear of Old Meg. Then Dafydd, white-faced and trembling found courage to speak. "Come with you I will. Nothing more have I to lose."

"Pray instead ..." Jencyn vainly tried to break in, but he could feel the spirit of the company against him. Perhaps indeed, they were right. If Old Meg were a witch, then she should be punished. No one should fear approaching her to mete out justice for that would be the will of the Lord. But they should have proof. . ..

"Proof we have had in plenty," retorted Morris ap Evan when Jencyn made his point. "But there is always the river. If she floats, she is guilty."

A murmur of agreement sprang from the assembly and arrangements were made for the men to meet early the following day.

"Bring pitch-forks and cudgels," advised Morris. "An old woman she may be, but don't forget, she has the Devil on her side."

At dawn the men congregated on the bank of the river and there was an angry excitement flowing through them which gave them courage to tread the path towards the old woman's cottage. The frustration of the months of self-denial overflowed into a surge of aggression which might previously have found expression in a wild football game, but which now formed the men into a noisy, threatening melee. With snatches of song and obscene jokes bolstering their mettle they took the path leading to the copse where Old Meg's hovel was hidden.

In the kitchen at Ty Celyn, Catrin wondered why the farm hands were not assembling for breakfast. Twm sat at the table supping at a bowl of butter-milk and he looked warily at Mari.

"Gone they are," the girl said, "gone to settle a score with Old Meg." She shivered. "A witch she is, Mistress Thomas and responsible for all our misfortunes."

"Who says?"

"Everyone says. Look at all the trouble ...."

"What will they do to her?"

Twm shrugged. "Jencyn says they must have proof ... but thinking I am that they will not take any notice of him when they get there."

Catrin caught her breath. She remembered the crone lying sick and cold on her straw bed, and the old woman's words, *"curses, or the fear of them bring me food."*

"She is no witch,"

Catrin grabbed her cloak and flinging it around

151

her shoulders ran to the stables for Sheba. Mari and Twm tried to call her back as she cantered through the yard, but Catrin took no notice. Hers would be a lone voice but she had to speak, nevertheless. The riverbank was deserted when she reached it but she caught up with the men as they neared the thicket of trees surrounding Old Meg's home.

"What do you think you are doing?" Catrin's voice rang out angrily and unusually shrill and she tried to calm Sheba who was rearing nervously as those men nearest her turned and approached aggressively.

"Jencyn," Catrin appealed. "Stop these men. Old Meg is no witch."

Jencyn caught hold of her bridle and attempted to lead Sheba away from the men who had pressed around Catrin with angry imprecations.

"If she is no witch, then we will soon have proof," he affirmed but Morris pushed him aside.

"Proof there is in plenty." His face was flushed and running with sweat; his eyes hard and determined. "Will we stay content to be cursed by Meg forever?" he appealed to the men. "Will we allow the Devil to work in our midst?"

Catrin watched helplessly as the group surged towards the cottage, but even the bravest quailed as they stood in the clearing before the front door.

"Come out, Old Meg," shouted Morris. "Come out, or it is breaking down your door we'll be."

One of the men threw a stone through the small window, splintering the wooden slats. A small black cat with lean ribs and mewing with hunger, sprang from a tree and was rewarded by a blow from a cudgel which spreadeagled the creature on the flagstones.

"Come on, boys. Are we going to wait forever?"

Dafydd joined Morris as the man flung himself against the door. Contrary to their expectation it fell easily into the small room, the rotten timber and rusted hinges no defence against their weight and fury. Then the cries of their supporters died on the lips as they watched the two men recoil, covering their faces with their arms as a protection from the stench which greeted them. Inside the hovel, the body of Old Meg, dead for weeks from disease and starvation, lay decomposing. The men stood silent, their excitement quenched and one by one they turned to walk back to the village, bewilderment and defeat written in their stance.

Alone, Catrin found herself shaking. Pity for Old Meg vied with relief that the old woman had not suffered the indignity and fright of the drowning which would have been hers if Death had not snatched her earlier. She found the hollow oppressive, the surrounding hills sombre and menacing, in spite of their dress of summer green, the song of the blackbird and the patter and chatter of woodland creatures, all impervious to the anguish and anxiety of human emotion. The valley had held such happiness for Catrin as a child. Only gradually had she learned that the beauty of the hills shed a deceptive veneer over the lives of the men and women who scratched a living on their slopes. Now, misfortune which dogged so many of her fellows, had cast its net about her too, transforming her terrain into something ominous, foreboding, pregnant with ill fortune. The *Valley of the Shadow* thought Catrin with a shudder and she wished for wings to fly away from her unhappiness, her loneliness, her fears. In that moment she felt herself, like Simon, a fugitive, fleeing from oppression and injustice.

Subdued and dejected, she took her time over the return journey to Ty Celyn, but when she arrived at the farmhouse, she found Mari waiting for her in the kitchen. The maid's eyes were bright, her manner secretive. She drew Catrin into a corner.

"Oh, Mistress," she whispered. "There is news I have for you, but no one else must hear it." She held out her palm on which lay a silver coin. "This I have been given for keeping my tongue still."

"Mari, what is it?" Catrin's blood had begun to pound as a wild hope rose within her breast.

"The gentleman, Mistress Thomas. That one that was here for a while. Waiting for you he is in the old barn."

Catrin drew in her breath, stunned, and the look she gave Mari was unbelieving, incredulous.

"The truth, I am telling you, Mistress. He really is there."

Mari held up the coin again as proof positive that her message was genuine.

"Bless you, Mari. Tell no one." Catrin clasped the girl's hands in a gesture of gratitude, then ran towards the door. She collided with Jencyn who was entering. He looked at her slyly. "In a hurry, Mistress Thomas?"

Catrin paused and forced herself to compose her features. "Not at all. I'm just going to see how the hens are sitting. No hurry there is about that little job."

Catrin held her head high as she left the kitchen, and walked discreetly until she was well clear of the farmyard. Then she ran breathlessly, oblivious of the stones in her path, the briars which threatened from the hedges, the hillside which rose steeply, making her gasp with effort. A chestnut mount was tethered near the barn and as Catrin approached he whinnied and snorted restlessly.

The door of the barn opened and the girl stood still, her pulse pounding as Simon appeared, his arms stretched out towards her.

"My little Kate!"

"You came." Catrin found herself pressed close to Simon's firm frame and felt his breath warm on her cheek as his lips found hers. "I was so afraid that I would never see you again."

"I pray that we shall never be parted long."

He drew into the safety of the barn and they clung together without speaking, timelessly soothing hurt and fulfilling need. With gentle fingers, Simon stroked Catrin's forehead, her cheeks, her breasts; he kissed away the tears wet on her cheek, the beads of sweat on her forehead. For blissful moments they forgot the threat of the outside world as each gained solace from the other, expressing a love which was at the one time both tranquil and passionate.

"I have longed for you, Catrin. During those weeks of hiding, when everything seemed lost, you were the star on which the course of my life was set."

"Will you take me with you?"

"I cannot. I will return when I have made a new

life in a new country. When I can offer you a home, then I will come for you."

"You are going to France?"

"No. My only future there would be soldiering. I have no wish to spend my life in killing; in fighting other people's wars. At first I thought I had no option but to do so, but I waited. The weeks and months trickled by as the men in Newgate were one by one hanged or sentenced to transportation. Some of them were going to the New World as convicts, and the longing grew inside me to go too, but as a free man." Simon's face grew animated and a new hope shone in his eyes. "I have a little money, hidden by my father. It is enough to buy my passage and to save me from starvation when I arrive. I will work and save sufficient to set up a homestead and then I will return for you."

"Will you not be in danger there too?"

"Not with my new name-Johnson; and not in Maryland. There are many Catholics there and they will not wish to ask questions. Catrin, will you wait for me?"

"Forever if need be."

"Not for ever. Please God, let it not be forever." Simon buried his face in Catrin's hair. "I must go now. Immediately to the Morrises of Llantarn near Merthyr. They are enquiring about a ship which is to leave soon from Bristol. They are trustworthy people, Catrin, and any message I may send from America will reach you through them. It will be safer for you that way."

Once more he drew her close, this time with the ardour and anguish of parting. Then Catrin stood alone, her face pallid, her emotions turbulent with joy and sadness, hope and despair. She listened as horse shoes struck against the stones of the hill-track, dry now with the drought of summer, and then smoothing her dishevelled hair ran down to the farm.

Jencyn was repairing a water-butt when she stepped into the yard and the glance he threw her was close but cursory. Catrin entered the kitchen with relief that she had been unobserved.

She would not have been so complacent if she had known that earlier Jencyn had been in the stable when Simon had spoken to Mari and that he had witnessed their transaction. Simon, at first concealed behind an out-house, had waited until Mari had stepped outside to throw some meal to the hens. The men, returned from their witch-hunt, were taking advantage of the fine day to work in the fields and when Simon drew her attention and stepped into view he had believed that they were alone. Jencyn, from the shadowy confines of the stable could see him clearly. He recognised the dark suit, the blond hair, the straight chin. After his encounter with Catrin he had followed discreetly, watching her run across the fields and disappear into the barn. His lips curved. There was now sufficient reason for him to pay a visit to Mr. Evans.

"To Llantrisant market I am going tomorrow," he told Jenette that evening. "My business will take all day."

Jenette spooning broth from the iron pot over the fire did not immediately reply. Her cheeks were pinched. Although she reckoned it to be early, she had been having pains for some hours.

"Near my time I am," she told him. "The baby will be born tomorrow."

Jencyn's face darkened. He had no intention of altering his plans. "I'll see that the women know. You will not be alone." He sipped from his bowl. "This broth is too salty," he complained. "You must keep your mind on your tasks, Jenette. Remember, Godliness is fostered by hard work and thrift."

The girl sighed. There was no pleasing Jencyn. The broth was either too thick or too thin, the room untidy, his socks lumpy with darns. Jenette no longer worked at the farmhouse, but her husband was a harder task-master than Mrs. Thomas had ever been.

"I thought I saw Mr. Johnson today." Jencyn kept his voice casual but he looked sharply at Jenette as he spoke. "The map-maker. In the farmyard he was. Asking for Mistress Thomas."

"Perhaps he has come back for his sword."

"Sword?"

Jenette had spoken thoughtlessly but Jencyn's reaction frightened her. He put down his bowl and stood, alert and demanding.

"What sword?"

"I ... I ... don't know, Jencyn. The words were foolish. It's the pain..."

"You do know, Jenette. Tell me. Tell me you must!" The man's eyes blazed and Jenette, drained by the dragging ache in her back, weakened.

"In Mistress Catrin's chest. I saw it. And a coat. A fine coat. Finer it was than any even Mr. Evans wears."

"A sword and a fine coat! What would a map-maker do with items such as these?" Jencyn relaxed and a complacent smile spread across his features. "Sit, Jenette and finish your supper. Profit you have given us today. Profit and fortune."

Jencyn determined to rise early in order to finish his business at the market in time to call at Ynysbedw on the way back. Fate decreed otherwise. All night Jenette rolled with pain and the woman called from the village waited helplessly. In the morning Catrin arrived at the cottage and told Jencyn that she had sent Twm to the market. "You may be needed here," she told him.

Jencyn strode out angrily to the fields nearby where he worked all the morning, listening to the screams which came frequently from the small cottage.

At noon, Catrin called him. "You have a son," she told him, but her smile was nervous, and the look she threw at him dubious and uncertain.

The man put down his scythe and wiping his brow entered the dark building, smokey and hot from the fire, necessary for cooking but uncomfortable in the rising June temperature.

Jenette lay exhausted on the low bed, her face ashen and drawn.

"You are well, wife?" Jencyn asked. He forebore to stoop and kiss her. Instead, he turned to the cradle which stood by the side of the bed and looked down at the infant inside. The baby screwed up his face and wailed, his tightly clenched fists beating against the air. The child's complexion was fair; his hair a fiery red.

Jencyn's heart contracted within him. The infant

was a living reminder of Dic, his handsome, virile, shepherd father. Jencyn remembered the way Jenette had looked at Dic; the way she had turned to him with open gestures of love. The same gift had not been awarded to him. The girl still shrank from him, avoided his embrace. Although Jencyn could satisfy his immediate need, there was an elusive longing which had been denied.

His face hardened as he turned from the cradle. "This is the child of sin," he announced, and before Jenette could protest, "I have promised to nurture him, and nurture him I will. I will provide food, shelter and clothing. But we will have other children, Jenette, sons and daughters, and he will serve them. That way we shall save his soul for God."

He left the cottage and Catrin cooled Jenette's hot brow with water. "Try not to worry," she comforted. "But 'tis a pity that your baby did not have black hair."

Four days passed before an opportunity to leave the farm and visit Ynysbedw presented itself to Jencyn. He found Griffith Evans sunning himself on a rustic bench in the flower garden. Incongruously canopied by roses, the man sprawled with legs wide apart, a snore emanating from his open mouth.

Jencyn coughed discreetly and Evans started in surprise, dusting the stale tobacco from his coat.

He was alert immediately. "You have something to tell me, Jencyn?"

"How am I to know that what I tell will not harm my Mistress in some way?" Jencyn looked at Evans pensively. Although the other man would not have believed it, he was quite serious. Jencyn's conscience required reasons for his actions. He needed

160

justification for any deed which might bring misfortune to others.

"Now am I likely to do anything to bring distress, *more* distress to such a lovely creature?" Evans waved Jencyn to a seat facing him. "I assure you that my actions are only designed to help her. Regard her position, Jencyn. Would you not agree that she is in need of a protector? Someone to manage her affairs? Any information you are likely to bring will only serve her interests."

Jencyn still hesitated.

"Surely you realise, man, that my design is not entirely philanthropic. You share your bed. What of mine?"

If Jencyn had been more used to levity he would have smiled. The information did not come as any surprise but he had needed it spelled out. The implications too did not elude him. With Catrin Thomas safely married to Evans, a tenant would be needed for Ty Celyn. Who better than himself? He was aware of the dangerous political overtones of his news, particularly where it concerned Jenette's disclosures, but he rightly surmised that Evans needed a weapon. His mistress would not easily surrender her future to the gross, elderly man seated opposite him, even though it was for her own long term good. In the circumstances he had no hesitation in telling what he knew of Simon's visit or recounting Jenette' information.

"You say that this sword is in the girl's chest?"

"Together with a richly embroidered coat."

Evans' face folded in lines of satisfaction. "So a further search by Willoughby and his men would reveal unhappy evidence!"

"You are not thinking ...."

"Of course not, man. I am only interested in politics as far as they serve me. What are they for else?"

Rising he pushed his hand into his pocket and drew out a coin for Jencyn. "Go now." He dismissed the man cursorily. "When this business is finished you will be well rewarded."

Alone, Evans lit his pipe reflectively. So Catrin Thomas had become involved with the Jacobite cause. Truly, she was following the tradition of her family for fastening on to the losing side. Her actions mattered little providing the knowledge did not become public property, and indeed, if the facts led to the arrest of the rebel, he could arrange for the girl to be honoured as a result. Possibly she had developed a frivolous attachment to the wanted man, but Evans did not put a great store of importance on this possibility. Catrin had been well brought up and would have done nothing foolish. She would soon see sense when her position was explained to her.

He decided to waste no time, but to visit Catrin at the first opportunity. Not on the morrow as he had business to attend to at Llantrisant, but possibly on the following day. He smiled with satisfaction. The girl could not possibly refuse him now.

ELEVEN

Jencyn journeyed back to Ty Celyn well pleased with his day's transaction. The coin pressed in his hand by Griffith Evans lay safely buttoned in his pocket, ready to be placed with its fellows, those earned in the same way, and those saved over the years by dint of self-denial and hardship. Jencyn kept them in a metal box which he had hidden away in the chimney-piece. No one, not even Jenette, knew of the existence, of this store, the nucleus of what Jencyn hoped and intended would one day become a fortune.

The work at the farm attended to and his market purchases and transactions accounted for, he crossed the fields to his cottage.

Jenette was feeding the baby when he pushed open the door. She stood nervously, the baby still attached to her nipple, and spooned broth into a wooden bowl. Jencyn took it to the rough board which served as table and as he sipped he nodded appreciatively.

"Good is this, wife," he remarked and Jenette's eyes opened wide with surprise at the unexpected praise. She could not know that today, even the sight of the red-headed infant suckling at his wife's breast was unable to disturb the feeling of warm satisfaction which imbued his limbs.

"Our fortunes are in the making," he continued,

unable to resist the temptation of talking about his ambitions. "Soon it is out of this cottage we shall be. A farm we shall have, *Mrs. Davies.* This day have I been to see Mr. Griffith Evans."

Jenette's lips slackened with dismay. "What have you done, Jencyn? What did you tell him?" The memory of her revelations concerning the coat and the sword stabbed through her, rousing fear for her mistress. "I want no harm to come to anyone. What I said I will deny."

"And what use will that be when evidence there is to support your words? Rest assured, wife. No harm will come to Mistress Thomas. Looking for a wife is Mr. E vans and this will solve many problems for your precious mistress. How else do you think she will manage if she does not wed?"

Jenette turned from her husband. The baby had dropped off to sleep and she removed her nipple from his now flaccid gums and placed him in the cradle. A black cloud descended over her and she swallowed hard to prevent the tears pricking at her eyes from running down her cheeks. So Mistress Catrin was to suffer the same fate that had been meted out to her. She too would be obliged to marry a man who only filled her with revulsion. Like the other servants she had taken note of the lecherous glances Griffith Evans threw in Catrin's way, and had seen also the hastily suppressed alarm which sprang in the girl's eyes whenever Evans spoke to her. There had been much talk among the maid-servants and they all hoped that Catrin would be able to send him packing and that a younger more personable suitor would arrive to be master of Ty Celyn.

Sitting back in his chair, Jencyn waited for Jenette to fill his mug with ale. She splashed it into the container resentfully. During the months since her marriage, the edge had worn from the initial relief and gratitude she had felt when Jencyn had offered her his protection. Her own natural ebullience was uneasily suppressed and as the days and weeks passed, Jencyn's exacting ways, his sermonising and his interminable prayers became more tedious. They contrasted oddly with his brief but fiery moments of clumsy passion. Jenette submitted to what she was assured was her duty with a dull ache for Dic's playful love-making.

The arrival of Huw, her baby, roused hitherto unfelt emotions inside her. The small, red-headed infant provoked intense maternal instincts, summoning all her loyalty and protection. Jencyn's cold words concerning the child martialled these feelings into a determined defence, and transformed the indifference and irritation she felt for her husband into something akin to hatred. How could her child be tainted with sin? She had loved Dic truly, and if her baby was a reminder of her lover's body with his flaming hair and strong limbs, she was glad.

The following day Catrin called at the cottage. She brought some butter and a warm cover for the cradle. The baby clenched her finger tightly as she bent over him in admiration.

"He is a blessing. Remember that. How are you feeling, Jenette?"

"Very well, Mistress Catrin. I am strong." Jenette paused. She could not find words to tell her mistress how sick she felt in spirit. She wanted too to warn

165

Catrin about her disclosures to Jencyn, but felt too ashamed to confess. She sighed. "Plenty of milk I have got for the little one. I must be thankful."

Catrin looked at her uneasily as she took her leave and the girl bobbed in respect. Jenette did not wear the same happy face that had been her hall-mark during the time she was in service at Ty Celyn. The shadow of a future with a husband not of her own choosing hung over her with unrelieved gloom.

As Catrin picked her way across the fields back to Ty Celyn, she determined that her own life would follow a different pattern. There was no reason why, until she heard once more from Simon, she could not make a success of the farm. She had learnt much from her father and brothers about husbandry, and the hands were good and reliable. She must have news soon from the drover who had promised to sell the necklace and then she would be able to tell Griffith Evans that she would be able to meet her debts in a reasonable time. Whatever happened she vowed never to accept Evans as husband. She shuddered at the thought, and on reaching the farm threw on an apron and helped Mari with the churning in the buttery. The hard work helped to keep her fears at bay.

The afternoon was to bring her good news. Soon after the mid-day meal, when the hands were back in the fields and when by good fortune Jencyn was attending to cattle in the furthest pasture, Mr. Wilson, the drover called. Tethering his horse at the gate, he strode through the farmyard singing loudly, his wide-brimmed hat tilted on his head at a rakish angle. He had just finished a very satisfactory assignment. The world was good and the sun shone. His job at Ty

Celyn completed he was going to renew his acquaintance with a plump widow who lived just outside Cardiff.

"Ask Mr. Wilson into the parlour, Mari."

Catrin had watched his arrival through the kitchen window, and now she hastened into the house and straightened her bodice and smoothed her hair. Her fingers were trembling and she could hardly bear to hear the news in case it brought disappointment.

"Your servant, Ma'am." Mr. Wilson bowed stiffly as he entered the room. "If you remember I had a little transaction to attend to for you."

"Did ... did you ... ?"

Mr. Wilson winked and tapped the side of his nose. "You asked the right man, Ma'am. Nick Wilson knows a thing or two about the world. There is a rich merchant of my acquaintance ..." He paused complacently. The job had pleased him. It had been a change from his usual errands of exchanging letters or delivering sums of money. It had given him the opportunity of calling at one of Bristol's finest houses. As he had anticipated, the rich merchant he approached quibbled at nothing to please the young and spoilt wife who sat at his side, bored and fretful. Her expression changed when Nick Wilson drew the necklace from his pocket. She held out her hands and the rubies glittered over her pale skin with liquid flame and she touched the antique gold with undisguised delight.

"La, husband, this trifle pleases me." She draped the chaplet around her slim neck and stood admiringly before a glass. "I must have it."

Mr. Wilson had no hesitation in quoting a

hundred and eighty guineas as his price, and the merchant watching the pendulous jewels falling like drops of warm blood on his wife's rising breasts had no hesitation in paying.

Now the driver pulled a bag from his pocket and showered gold coins on to the table in front of Catrin. "One hundred and seventy guineas," he announced. "I have already taken my share."

The girl ran her hand through the pile of coins. The bright gold trickled through her fingers, and her dream sprang back vividly into her mind. She remembered how the acorns showering from the trees had changed first to rubies and then to gold. Her spirits rose. The message had been clear. She was right to sell the trinket, even though her family had guarded it for so many generations.

"Thank you, Mr. Wilson. You have done well. Will you refresh yourself with food or drink before you leave?"

"A glass of ale perhaps. I'll ask one of the gels in the kitchen, Ma'am on my way out." He bowed and left, his mind already on the food and home comforts which awaited him at the pretty widow's house.

Catrin filled the embroidered pocket she wore at her waist with the coins and then ran upstairs to her room to place them in the wooden casket which still contained the statue. She hid the box in the bottom of her oak chest, beneath Simon's decorated coat. She smoothed the fine cloth as she did so and remembered how her fingers had touched Simon's cheek and fondled his hair and how their love had swelled and encompassed them. Where was Simon now? If his ship had not sailed yet, he was probably still in hiding with his friends at Llantarn. Perhaps he would be able to call on her on his way to the coast. The upsurge of delighted hope was quickly quenched by Catrin's realization of the dangers involved. No one had suspected his earlier visit; it would be too much to hope that such good fortune would be theirs a second time.

Catrin dropped a kiss on to the velvet fabric before closing the chest. Her heart was loving and hopeful. Simon would be back one day and she would wait for him, if necessary, for years. The gold coins in the wooden box had given her the freedom to do so.

The following day she called on Morgan Howell, the curate. He looked at her curiously, wondering why the sparkle had suddenly re-appeared in her eyes, the happy flush on her cheeks.

"Looking well, you are, Mistress Thomas," he told her and bade his wife bring them some refreshment.

To Catrin's surprise, Mrs. Howell took a small wooden box from the dresser and unlocked it carefully. With pride she showed Catrin the tea inside and with great ceremony brewed a spoonful in a special pot.

"A present from my sister," she explained. "Doing well is her husband. In law, he is. A great friend of the Bishop."

Catrin sipped the expensive liquid finding it oddly soothing. She thought of Simon and supposed that he would drink a great deal of tea when he reached the Americas. The idea both comforted her and made her feel particularly poignant at the thought of their long parting.

Over the tea, she made polite conversation, but her cup empty, she shifted uncomfortably. "I wanted some advice," she began, and glanced from clergyman to wife with nervous speculation.

Mrs. Howell collected the cups. "Leave you then I will." She threw a wan smile in Catrin's direction. Her own daughter was not much older, and since the girl had married and gone to live in Swansea, she missed her a great deal.

Alone with the clergyman, Catrin bit her lip and wondered how to begin. She was encouraged by the homely way Mr. Howell's wig was perched awry on his furrowed brow, and the frayed cuffs of his drab coat reminded the girl that poverty was no stranger to the man's household. Somehow this made it easier for her to confide her worries concerning her debts, and to ask the curate if he could tell her where she could find out how much stock she would have to sell to pay Evans in full.

"It may not be necessary," she added, reminding herself that it was always possible that when she paid the hundred and seventy guineas Mr. Evans might agree to wait for the rest. "I have therefore to be discreet."

"Trust me." Mr. Howell looked at the girl sitting in front of him, so vulnerable, yet so determined. He too, was reminded of his daughter and felt impelled to help the girl if it was at all possible. "I'll make enquiries for you myself and let you know in a few days what I have discovered. I will take great care," he assured her. "No one will suspect that I am investigating on your behalf."

Catrin left the house feeling relieved and

comforted. Mr. Howell would do his best for her she felt sure, and as she returned to Ty Celyn her heart was in tune with the warm sun which shone down on the valley benevolently, encouraging a profusion of blossoms in the hedgerows, touching with pale gold the rich green of the serrated leaves of the oak, and the more delicate draperies of the ash trees which hugged the lower slopes of the hills and straddled across field and meadow.

The mood stayed with her throughout the week, mellowing the household, easing the lot of the maids busy in dairy and kitchen, bringing jokes to the lips and smiles to the faces of the boys in the farmyard, bidding the spinning-wheel turn with a happy song and the knitting needles click merrily. When Mr. Howell called on her to tell her that the money she needed could be raised without denuding Ty Celyn of too much stock or losing a great deal of land, her spirits rose further. She would be able to challenge Mr. Evans when he called, knowing that he could hold no great threat over her head.

She did not have to wait long. Two days later, a strident voice in the farmyard told her that Griffith Evans was ordering the stable-lads around, bidding them take care of his horse. She, hastened into the parlour and when her visitor was announced she was sitting in the window-seat diligently working on an embroidered apron. As she rose to drop a curtsey, she flattered herself that the agitation which made her heart pound vigorously did not show in her face.

"Good-afternoon, Mr. Evans." Catrin sat again and resumed her task on the silken material. "What brings you in this direction today?"

A smirk spread over Evans' jowl as he sat heavily on a chair which faced the girl. His eyes, puffy-lidded, glinted complacently as he drew a chased snuff box from his pocket. He sniffed noisily with each nostril, leaving a trail of fine dust over his kerseymere waistcoat and lacy cravat. Catrin noticed that he wore new shoes with fine silver buckles. She shivered inwardly. Mr. Evans was dressed to go a-wooing.

"Come now, Mistress Thomas. I think you know what brings me in your direction." Griffith Evans leaned towards the girl confidentially. "I'm sure that you haven't forgotten our little talk - about your debts - about my proposition."

"And I am equally sure that you can remember my reply."

"In detail, my dear Mistress Thomas. But isn't it usual to rebuff a suitor at the first approach?"

Catrin turned cool, confident eyes towards her visitor. "If you think that, Mr. Evans, you are deluding yourself. I can assure you that my answer remains the same now as then. You cannot hold the threat of your mortgage on this farm over my head. I have the means to pay you in full."

Evans' eyes narrowed. Catrin's words were what he had expected to hear. He had no idea how the girl had managed to solve her financial problems, although he hazarded a guess that her new fortune was somehow bound up with Jenette's revelation concerning the coat and sword. He suspected that the girl had become involved with the Jacobite cause. Perhaps this money had been deposited with her for safe keeping. If so, then he held even more Aces in his hand.

"What a pity it is then," he began with a slow smile, "that the Justices will exact such a heavy penalty from you when you come before them for harbouring a Jacobite fugitive. It should account for most of the money you have acquired to pay off your debts." He paused, noting the way Catrin's cheeks had paled, recognising the panic in her eyes, noticing her fingers, frozen into immobility over the silken threads. He had gambled, putting his suspicions into words, and he had won. "I am sure," he went on steadily, "that my influence will ensure that you do not have to suffer more severe punishment-such as imprisonment, or transportation."

Catrin felt the silence in the room as he waited for her reply, to be almost tangible. This was how the fox must feel when cornered by the hounds. Griffith Evans could not tear her flesh but he was effectively shattering her dreams.

"You are talking nonsense, Mr. Evans." Tight-lipped, she determined to put up a spirited defence. "You are trying to intimidate me without cause."

"I think not, Mistress Thomas. I do not speak without evidence. There is a certain coat ... and a sword ..."

Jenette, thought Catrin. Somehow or other Jencyn had wormed the information out of her. "I don't know what you mean ..."

"I think you do, young lady. Witnesses can speak against you."

"I'll pay the fine. I'll risk transportation. You still can't make me marry you. I'll go to prison first." Catrin stood now, her eyes blazing, fury bringing a flush to her skin.

Griffith Evans felt desire swell as he watched the passionate rise and fall of the girl's breasts, imperfectly concealed by her gauze fichu. Catrin's reluctance to share his bed did not trouble him. He blindly believed that his persistence would pay off in the end. His arrogant assumption that he was in fact doing the girl a favour by making his offer convinced him that eventually she would be a grateful and dutiful wife.

"Then there was the visit of a certain Mr. Johnson."

Catrin flinched. "A cartographer, sir. He was stranded here during the bad weather."

"Then what of his visit a fortnight ago? Captain Willoughby will be very interested to hear all this evidence."

"What are you implying?"

"That your Mr. Johnson is a Jacobite on the run, and one word from me will set the ball rolling for his capture."

Catrin turned and gazed through the window. Outside, the sun shone on roses and lavender, bushes which seemed to inhabit a different world. A thrush perched on an apple tree sang lustily. Bird and flower were free; their battles with the elements, not with their own kind. It was left to man to subdue his fellows, to impose his will on those too weak to resist, to greed after riches, to lust for power.

Griffith Evans stood behind the girl and placed his hands on her shoulders. He turned her to face him and she felt his onion breath, warm on her cheek.

"I think you'll see that my way is the best way,"

he told her. "I am not concerned with politics. It worries me not a jot whether your Mr. Johnson is free or in prison. But unless you agree to me arranging a date with the parson and drawing up a marriage settlement, it is behind bars he will be, and your future a very different one from that which I am offering you."

Catrin recoiled from the smile of triumph which crooked the man's fleshy lips. If she could be sure that Simon had left the country ... even so, Evan's pique might be such that the width of the Atlantic would prove no obstacle to his revenge.

"Go and see Morgan Howell then. You offer me no choice." Catrin twisted from the man's grasp and threw him a glance of hostile contempt.

Evans relaxed. He dusted his waistcoat and straightened his wig. "I am glad you see it my way, my dear." He lifted the girl's hand and patted it paternally. He was wise enough to resist the urge to draw her into his arms. There would be time enough for that. Soon there would be an end to waiting for the favours of love, and he had little doubt that his blandishments would eventually turn Catrin into a willing bride. "I shall see Mr. Howell on my way home, and tomorrow I shall visit my lawyer. The following day I will be back with the settlement for you to sign."

Catrin managed to keep her face immobile until the man left. Then she ran upstairs and flung herself on to her bed in a paroxysm of weeping. She had vowed to wait for Simon, no matter how many years passed until their next meeting. Now she was being forced to break that vow - and for Simon's sake.

175

"I would have suffered anything myself," she breathed, "but I cannot let Simon go to the gallows. Simon! Simon! Will you ever understand when you learn what has come between us?"

Eventually she splashed water on her face and tried to hide some of the blotches around her eyes by applying a little of the ointment made from cowslip flowers which her mother had always kept by to preserve the skin. When she returned to the kitchen she pretended a heartiness she did not feel.

The servants looked at her curiously. As he left the building, Mr. Evans had announced that he was to marry their mistress, but the red rims around the girl's eyes which all the ointment in the world could not conceal, warned them against making any remarks.

The following morning she had a visit from Mr. Howell, anxious because he knew instinctively that the marriage was not of Catrin's choosing. Catrin refused to be drawn.

"You gave me good advice," she told him. "Unfortunately I am still obliged to wed Mr. Evans."

"If it is still a question of money ...."

"Money is not involved now, Mr. Howell. I am unable to explain, but I have decided that my best course of action is to marry Mr. Evans." She looked at the curate boldly. "After all, I shall have a life of ease, with many luxuries. Many women would sell themselves for less."

Mr. Howell threw her a disbelieving glance. Catrin was, he knew, not the sort of woman who would sell herself for any price. He felt glad at that moment that his own daughter was married to a man of her own choosing, even though at the time of her marriage he had harboured doubts as to his son-in-law's suitability.

"There is nothing more to be said." Catrin rose and showed the curate out. She was being discourteous in not offering him hospitality, but her taut feelings threatened to overcome her. Had he stayed longer, she would have broken down and perhaps disclosed emotions and motives which were better hidden.

As she watched the clergyman leave the farmyard on his bedraggled mount, Catrin felt that the house, the stables, the countryside, had taken on a nightmare quality. She could not believe that she was the same person as the girl who had loved Simon and waved him away with rich promises of hope, who had welcomed the return of the drover and received the gold coins - the key to freedom. Her dream must have been a fiction, conjured up by desire and longing. Perhaps there was no box, no statue, no necklace, no coins. She felt lost, unable to find a secure foothold in the present or the future.

Did Simon exist? Had her life been a mirage? She ran to her room and flung open the oak chest. It was a relief to lift out the velvet coat and to handle the sharp steel of the sword. Simon was real, and so was her love for him. The wooden casket was real too. She held the worn statue, dark with the age of centuries, and let the coins trickle through her fingers; those coins which had promised her so much but which had proved so impotent.

Nevertheless gold was powerful; it would hold strength and influence away from the valley, away

177

from Griffith Evans. Catrin caught her breath at the enormity of the idea which suddenly encompassed her. An idea which would need courage and resourcefulness. An idea which developed and grew and became more feasible with every moment.

Away from the valley, gold would be able to buy her food and shelter. It would enable her to go to London and wait for Simon's return there. A message from Mr. Morris of Llantarn would reach her there as surely as if she were at Ty Celyn. What she would do in London, what her money would be worth, she had no idea. Perhaps she could take a position as a servant. Better still, as a governess, if she could prove her skills with letters.

Fired by the wonderful goal of freedom, Catrin found needle and thread and painstakingly began to sew the coins in the hems and seams of her homespun gown. Her needle worked quickly and all the while she made plans for her departure. She would wait until the day of her wedding as this would give Simon the opportunity of quitting the country before any hue and cry was raised. She would leave the farm in the morning, just before dawn, taking one of the lesser horses for Sheba would be too easy to trace. Her first call would be to Llantarn to speak to Mr. and Mrs. Morris. They would give her news of Simon, tell her when his ship was likely to reach Maryland.

The hem of her dress grew stiff and bulky as Catrin's agile fingers hid her fortune. A few coins she reserved for her pocket, but when she had finished her task, her gown was weighty. Catrin's spirits lightened. Now that they were not needed for her debts, what could she not do with the gold coins. She might even buy a passage to America!

Catrin gasped with excitement. Simon's ship would have already left, but there would be others. She would make her way to Bristol or London and wait until she found a vessel which would take her across the sea to a new life and a future with the man she loved!

TWELVE

When Griffith Evans arrived with his lawyer and the marriage settlement, he found Catrin strangely acquiescent. She appended her signature to the document without fuss although her fingers trembled around the quill and her cheeks held little colour.

Evans smiled complacently as the lawyer folded the parchment. He had expected some trouble, some argument about detail, some astringent words reflecting Catrin's spirited defence. Instead the girl's eyes were downcast, her demeanour one of decorous submission. Evidently she had thought over her future and decided that her best fortune lay as mistress of Ynysbedw.

"And now, my dear, see what I have brought you."

Griffith Evans opened parcels carried by his servant and showed Catrin a length of grey silk and another of quilted blue, sprigged with embroidered flowers. Another parcel contained fine lace and a length of muslin.

"For your wedding dress," Evans explained. "I have arranged for a tailor to call tomorrow to make it up for you. There is very little time for the wedding will take place two weeks today."

Catrin thanked him with little enthusiasm and when the tailor arrived, submitted dully to the various fittings. In spite of the unpopularity of the marriage, a great deal of excitement was engendered in the kitchen and Mari and Jane, handling the expensive fabrics and chatting with the tailor as they served his meals, wondered if Catrin was not being wise after all.

The tailor stayed for three days, during which time he not only completed Catrin's dress but attended to various other tasks in the household, repairing the curtain which hung in the parlour, and making petticoats for the servant girls. An atmosphere of charged excitement hung over Ty Celyn, not least because in spite of Catrin's obvious reluctance to discuss plans concerning the wedding arrangements, and her unwillingness to talk about the catering for the expected visitors, there was an air of happy and determined tension about her.

"If I didn't know how little she cares for Mr. Evans," Mari remarked in the kitchen one evening, "I would say that Mistress Thomas was very happy indeed."

Mari was not to know that each night Catrin lay in bed dreaming about her own plans. Mature reflection had warned her that leaving Ty Celyn on the day of her wedding would be unwise. A search party would immediately be summoned and the chances were that she would be found and have to face the consequences of Griffith Evans' undoubted anger.

So three days before the date fixed for her wedding, Catrin rose before dawn and donned the simple homespun gown which concealed her fortune. She realised that she would only be able to take the minimum of clothing with her and so had originally intended to take her useful green riding habit to supplement her everyday dress. Now, on sudden impulse, she removed it from the bundle she had gathered together, and substituted the new silk gown. As well, she took with her the wooden casket containing the statue, and which now housed also a brooch and rings which had belonged to her mother.

She crept from the house before sunrise and quietly saddled Polly, a good tempered pony, who, although not swift was nevertheless strong and reliable. The horse snorted and gave a low whinny as Catrin pulled at the straps and the girl stroked the beast's nose and whispered in her ear to calm her. Catrin started in alarm, her heart pounding as she heard, or imagined she heard, someone moving near the door, but when she led Polly outside, she found the farmyard apparently deserted. She paused at the farm gates and looked back at the house, her heart a riot of emotion. The sturdy building had been the centre of her life; had offered her a childhood full of happiness and laughter. Only recently had it become a place of sorrow, of fear, of foreboding. Had the stones suddenly become hostile, or was it that they had completed their task of nurturing the Thomas family and were sending its sole remaining representative into the unknown? Strangely, as she left, Catrin felt a blessing descend on her, as if the shades of her ancestors, the building, the living farm, the valley itself was sending her on a mission, as an emissary to spread the warmth of her upbringing and the strong resolution of her background into the world outside.

She turned quickly, her introspection becoming oppressive, then cantered along the riverbank. Polly took the rise to Penrhys slowly when they came to it, and Catrin paused on the summit to watch the rising sun bring the hills and the valleys to life, lighting leaf and fern with streaks of clear gold. She descended into the valley of the Rhondda Fach and fording the stream, found a trail which climbed towards the ridgeway which would take her north. This was new terrain for Catrin, but she had pored over the maps with Simon and she felt confident that she was on the right path. The rough road, widened somewhat after the assault by the early summer's droves of cattle which had been brought down regularly for market, wound through forest and straddled bleak hill-tops for dusty miles. When it dipped towards the valley of the Cynon and Catrin saw the tiny hamlet of Aberdare nestling in a crook of the river, she paused to refresh herself with a draught of home-made wine and a hunk of bread.

She hesitated to call on any cottage lest she should draw attention to herself and thereby enlighten any pursuers, but once through the small village, a fork in the road brought her face to face with fellow travellers. The small cortege was led by a middle-aged man who looked at Catrin with suspicion. Behind him, riding pillion and mazy from sleep for it was still early in the morning, was a small girl. The man's wife and teenage son followed him on separate mounts.

There was a trace of fear, of guilt in their faces and this matching Catrin's own feelings, she was encouraged to ask directions.

"Am I on the right road to Llantarn?" she enquired.

The woman's eyebrows lifted in surprise and she threw a cautious glance at her husband.

"Who do you know at Llantarn?" he asked Catrin

warily.

"I seek a Mr. Morris."

Some of the suspicion cleared from his wife's face. "We are going there too," she informed Catrin. "As we had not met you before, we were alarmed ... we are always alarmed on these occasions in case anyone should ask why we are out together so early. Not that they happen often."

"Our name is Jones," her husband broke in. "We had a letter a week since to say that the Daily Memento would take place today. St. Peter and Paul's day. We have travelled ten miles so far. And you?"

"A fair way."

Catrin was deliberatively evasive. She was still mystified. What was this Daily Memento, and why were the strangers going to Llantarn? One thing was sure, she would now be able to reach her goal without trouble and she fell in gratefully at the rear of the party.

Llantarn House was a sizeable manor with several acres of good land. Mr. and Mrs. Morris were at the portico to greet their guests and as they dismounted, servants led the horses to the rear of the building. Catrin followed her new friends into a square oak panelled hall as Mrs. Morris fussed around them.

"Mr. Jones, Mrs. Jones, Elizabeth, Henry. You managed the long journey!"

"We did indeed, Mrs. Morris. A small price for Peter and Paul. And fair company we had for the latter part of the journey." Mr. Jones turned towards Catrin.

The hostess's face tightened with dismay. She

glanced nervously at her husband.

"We do not remember sending you a letter." Mr. Morris stood stiffly erect, his stance one of defence.

Before Catrin could reply a door leading from the hall opened and the girl gasped with amazement as Simon stepped through it.

"Catrin!"

With a couple of long strides he was beside her, clasping her closely to him, gazing into her face unbelievingly.

"I must be seeing mirages. Too much wine last night has made me light-headed, imagining fairy forms where nothing can exist. But I can touch you, dearest Catrin, and you do not feel like a dream."

"I am not a dream, Simon. I am truly here and ready to go with you wherever you wish to take me. I have money, Simon. Enough for my passage and more besides. But how are you still here? I imagined that your ship must have sailed many days ago."

"There were difficulties." Simon hesitated. "The ship at Bristol was being watched. Mr. Morris tells me that I must travel first to La Rochelle and make my way to America from there."

Mrs. Morris approached, her face warm and welcoming now that she knew who Catrin was. "Simon has told us about you," she informed the girl. "Forgive me for being suspicious, my dear, but we have to be very careful on these occasions."

"Father Davies is here," Simon explained. "He is going to say Mass, the "Daily Memento" as we call it in any correspondence."

Catrin hesitantly accompanied Simon into a large

room which had been turned into a temporary chapel. An altar on which two candles were burning had been improvised at one end of the room. Besides the Jones family and the Morrises and their servants, there was another family who had journeyed six miles to be present and an elderly man who had travelled alone. When Father Davies entered the room Catrin saw a man in his forties, thick-set with a stubborn set to his jaw.

"Introibo ad altare Dei ..."

The Latin words of the Mass washed over Catrin like a mysterious tide, but a tide made soothing by the obvious devotion of the participants in the celebration. For herself she was incredibly aware of the presence of Simon, kneeling at her side. If Heaven was about her, she believed that this must be the cause and in spite of her confusion at the alien nature of the service, she prayed that they might stay together always. Fate had been cruel to her during the last twelve months, but was surely not so bitter as to throw her together with Simon, only to part them once more.

Afterwards, a late breakfast was served in the long dining-room, and refreshed spiritually and physically, the visitors took their leave.

Only now did Catrin and Simon have the chance of a private conversation and even then it was hurried and consisted mainly of explanations. Catrin told Simon about her encounters with Griffith Evans and how he was attempting to blackmail her into marriage.

"How could I agree? I belong to you, Simon. I promised you that I would wait and so I decided to follow you. The money from the sale of the necklace gave me the freedom to do so, and now it will help us set up a household in the New World."

"There may be hardships," Simon warned. "Danger too, before we actually sail. Are you sure, Catrin, that you can risk everything for me?"

"Quite sure. There is nothing in the valley for me now. Our future lies together."

Simon clasped Catrin's small hand in his. "Bless you, Catrin, for coming into my life. May I speak to Father Davies? He could marry us before he leaves." He kissed her tenderly and the surge of hope and delight which swept through the girl transported her from the mundane world, making her light-headed and feeling as if she was floating high in heaven.

The arrival of Mrs. Morris, bustling into the room having ushered the last of the guests from the premises, brought her back to some sort of reality.

"You can help me tidy away," she told Catrin and led her back to the large room where the service had been held. Together they folded the white linen cloth which had covered the altar and took it upstairs together with the gilt crucifix, the candlesticks and the red robe worn by the priest. Mrs. Morris led the girl to her bedroom and they put everything away in a large oak chest.

The older woman handled the objects with loving care. "My sister sent me the crucifix and candlesticks," she told Catrin. "She lives in Dunkirk. She is a nun."

"A nun!"

"She has dedicated her life to God."

Catrin felt a certain chill. Loving Simon as she did the concept was one which repelled her and she was glad when they joined the others downstairs and the warm human contact brought her back to a reality which she could understand.

"You must meet Father Davies." Mr. Morris introduced her to the priest who, now that he was dressed soberly in coat and wig, looked like any other country gentleman, a little hopeful, a little weary, a little disillusioned.

He bent over Catrin's hand. "I have heard about you, and how you saved Lord Simon's life."

"I have told Father Davies too, how we love each other," added Simon. "Before he leaves later today, he has agreed to bless our marriage."

"You do realise that life may be difficult?" the priest warned Catrin. "Even though there are several Catholics in positions of authority in Maryland, it is still not entirely safe to profess the faith, and in marrying a Catholic you will take upon yourself disadvantages you would otherwise avoid."

"My place is with Simon." Catrin's voice was firm. "Faith or no faith. To me religion matters little."

The priest looked doubtful. "To Simon it matters a great deal."

"And Simon matters a great deal to me," rejoined Catrin. "For him I would risk any peril."

Father Davies' lips curved slightly and there was a trace of compassion in the glance he threw at the girl. He turned to Simon.

"You are a lucky man to have such a helpmate," he remarked.

Mrs. Morris surveyed Catrin's homespun gown, still dusty from her long ride. "We'll have to find you something else for this special occasion," she decided. "Come upstairs with me and I'll see what I can find."

"But I have a dress." Breathlessly Catrin remembered her sudden and illogical urge to bring her new gown with her. A servant had previously taken her bundle into the kitchen, and now Mrs. Morris ordered it to be taken upstairs.

The older woman helped Catrin into the elegant robe, arranging the grey silk folds to show the flower-sprigged petticoat to its best advantage. Catrin took care to sweep her hair high over her forehead, allowing the long glossy tresses to fall over her shoulder in long curls. Mrs. Morris found a lacy mantilla for her to drape over her head and shoulders, and they descended the stairs and then entered the room where Simon waited in the company of the priest and Mr. Morris.

Simon extended his arms to Catrin, and she put a trembling hand in his. Together they stood in front of the priest and murmured the words which would unite them all their days. The ring was Catrin's mother's, brought with her in the wooden casket and as Simon slipped it on her finger, she vowed that she would never remove it.

The wedding breakfast, being unexpected, was simple, but Mrs. Morris had ordered fowls to be roasted on the spit, and Mr. Morris brought out a bottle of good wine so that they could drink the health of the newly-wed couple. Afterwards, Father Davies was obliged to leave, and Catrin and Simon stood in the courtyard and watched him mount the nag which was to carry him on his lonely road to Brecon.

That night Catrin lay in a massive four-poster

beside Simon, and wrapped in his embrace wondered if she would suddenly wake to find herself back in Ty Celyn with her problems still weighty on her shoulders. She buried her face in Simon's shoulders and tangled her fingers in his hair. If this was a dream, it was one she would cling to for the rest of her life. She and Simon would wander through a fantasy world together, making light of any difficulties encountered, painting the future with promise and hope.

The first pale rays of the sun slanting through the window roused her to a reality which did indeed offer much. Simon was already up and dressed. He had warned her that they would have to leave early that day so that they could travel south to Cardiff where a ship would take them across to France.

"It was indeed merciful fortune which persuaded you to leave when you did," he told her. "I should have missed you else."

Mr. Morris had given them a tin trunk and Simon packed it with their belongings. The grey silk dress went inside as did a brown woollen gown, calico aprons and thread stockings which, when they met for breakfast, Mrs. Morris insisted that Catrin accepted from her.

"You may find it difficult to buy anything when you have left this country," she warned.

Simon laughed. "Have no fear, Mrs. Morris. Ships trade regularly with the Americas. I should not wonder if we will be better supplied than you are here in Merthyr."

"Nevertheless, Catrin must not arrive without a few good dresses. 'Tis a poor trousseau she has for a new bride."

Catrin leaned over and kissed the woman impulsively. "I could have had a fine trousseau and an old man," she declared. "I'll take Simon in the teeth of hardship."

A servant brought horses to the front of the house. There was a mount each for Simon and Catrin and a pack horse for their luggage. John, the servant, was to accompany them until they found other transport and then he was to bring the horses back.

"When you reach Newbridge, you should find farmers going south," Mr. Morris advised them. "You will easily be given a lift in a waggon."

For several miles, the small cortege followed the course of the river Taff, the road being little more than a track, necessitating them to follow each other in single file. They had started early in the day, so although the horses made slow progress it was still before noon when they reached the hamlet of Newbridge and the river widened and deepened as it met its tributary of the Rhondda.

They stopped here to rest the horses and to partake of the refreshments that Mrs. Morris had thoughtfully packed for them. Catrin felt the sun warm on her skin, the wine lively in her throat, the touch of Simon's hand on hers a tingling reminder of his nearness, and thought that she had never been so happy. Her ignorance of the geography of the neigh-bourhood masked from her the fact that only a couple of miles separated her from Ynysbedw and the wrath of Griffith Evans. So she was enabled to enjoy the sight of the dancing sunlight on the clear rippling river and to listen happily to the muted sound of the cascading falls at *Berw'r Rhondda,* the "salmon's leap".

As Mr. Morris had expected, it was not long before a waggon was found making its way to Cardiff. Catrin noticed it first, for they sat on a hillock which gave them a good view of the surrounding terrain. The waggon turned out of the yard of a farm a few hundred yards away and Catrin watched as the driver spoke to a man on horse-back who stood near the gate. She shivered suddenly as a chill ran down her spine for the black-coated rider reminded her forcibly of Jencyn.

"What is it, Catrin?" The girl had paled and Simon held her hand comfortingly.

She looked back at the farm gate, but the rider had disappeared and the waggon was approaching them.

"Nothing ... just something I imagined."

She forced a smile as the cart drew near, then the conversation with the driver and the red-cheeked laughing women who sat inside guarding round cheeses, distracted her attention.

Yes, they were going to Cardiff. "In a hurry we are," added the driver lugubriously. "Waiting all day I have been for these women to get themselves ready."

All the same he halted while Catrin and Simon took their leave of John and hoisted the tin trunk into the cart. Simon sat up front with the long-faced man while Catrin joined the women in the waggon. As they left a shadowy figure watched them silently from his hiding place in a copse of trees. He stood still while the waggon trundled south, then turning, he made his way back along the Rhondda river to Ynysbedw. Jencyn had news for Griffith Evans.

THIRTEEN

As Jencyn urged his horse toward Ynysbedw, relief washed over him. At last he had something positive to tell Griffith Evans. There was no mistaking his mistress or her escort. Few local men could match the height or the fairness of Mr. Johnson's complexion - if Johnson was indeed his name. A fortunate chance too had brought him into conversation with the farmer as the waggon had trundled out of the farmyard, for from it he learned the runaway's destination. This information should surely mitigate Evans' temper, might even show him that he, Jencyn, was not quite the dolt that he had been called when he had broken the news of his mistress' disappearance. In that despairing moment he had seen the tenancy of Ty Celyn slip from his grasp, he had felt pushed back to the mire and dung of the farm labourer, his ability and knowledge stifled and allowed to rot. And all for the whim of a stupid girl who did not know where her best fortune lay.

On the morning of her departure, Catrin's absence had not been quickly noted at Ty Celyn. Her morning duties were varied and took her to many different parts of the farm, so that anyone looking for her would assume that she was attending to a task elsewhere. It was not until after the men had been served with their mid-day meal that Mari became disquieted and spoke to Jane.

"Thinking I am that I have not seen the Mistress at all today."

Jane looked startled. "Now you mention it, neither have I," she replied. "Yet always she is here when we serve the food."

Mari ran upstairs to Catrin's bedroom. The bed was tidied, the window dosed tight; a strange atmosphere of emptiness hung over the chamber. She hesitated, then ran across to the oak chest and lifted the heavy lid. The grey silk dress, which she knew had been folded neatly inside, was missing. Mari's features were pale and guarded when she returned to the kitchen.

Jane meanwhile had gone outside into the yard and sought Twm. Mari joined them as they spoke together. Twm's face was close, as impenetrable as a nut.

"Not seeing her am I, neither," he added and looked slyly around at the outbuildings. The men were busy in the fields and would remain there for some hours. "Yet no need is there to raise any hue and cry at the moment."

"Is Sheba in the stables?" Mari peered across at the dark building.

"Sheba is there alright." Twm did not mention that Polly was missing.

"So she is not out riding." Jane's brows drew together anxiously. "Twm, we must look for her. She may have come to some harm."

"No harm is coming to Mistress Thomas. Not now. Go on with your work *merched*. Nothing is there to worry about."

196

Twm marched back to the barn his lips tightly shut, the information he had gleaned in the early hours of the day when a soft stirring in the stables had brought him out to investigate, firmly sealed inside him.

It was four o'clock in the afternoon when Jencyn, calling back at the farmhouse with a message for Catrin, found out that she was missing.

"Where have you looked?" he demanded of the maids and his voice held a strangely brutal quality.

"Twm said not to worry."

"And so you've done nothing - told no one?"

"What should we do? Who should we tell?"

The girls clung together, fearful of Jencyn's black looks, but cheekily resilient.

"Run away she has, I'll wager," said Jane. "And good luck to her."

"Run away I would too, if I had to marry old Mr. Evans," giggled Mari, but Jencyn did not stay to hear more. He strode over to the stables and threw a saddle on Sheba. At first the horse's presence had quieted his fears, but he quickly noticed that Polly was missing and was astute enough to understand Catrin's reasoning.

For the next two hours, in spite of the back-breaking work he had undertaken all the day, Jencyn scoured lane and field, questioning cottagers and labourers. His enquiries were fruitless and after calling at his own dwelling to revive himself with Jenette's soup, he knew that he had no recourse but to ride over to Ynysbedw and break the news to Griffith Evans.

As he expected, the effect was catastrophic.

Evans' already mottled face became even more suffused.

"Get out and find her, man," he roared. "Are you so stupid that you cannot find a chit of a girl?"

"Searching I have been for three hours," Jencyn retorted, "and now dusk is falling. Impossible it will be for me to continue this night."

"Then tomorrow you will start at dawn. You will search every corner of every wood and each inch of hillside. Impossible it is for her to have got very far, and no one in this neighbourhood will dare hide her while they know that I am looking for her. Ask everyone. Look everywhere. For her sake, man, if the concern you showed before isn't just hypocrisy. By God, I'll have the militia out if you don't bring her back soon, and then she'll have something to worry about!"

That night Jencyn's sleeplessness was back with him and he was up at dawn to saddle Sheba and ride up the river and down. The near impossibility of his task daunted him until, at noon, he made his startling discovery. There was an unusual flush in his cheeks when he was ushered into the parlour at Ynysbedw and confronted Evans with his news.

Griffith Evans, too, had slept little. The edge of his anger dulled, he was chagrined to find that he still wanted Catrin as much as ever. It was as if the girl had wound him in a mesh of frustrated desire and the more elusive she became, the more tormenting were the strands which bound him. Now this fellow was saying that she had gone to Cardiff, and not alone either. A man was with her.

"Bring her back," he ordered. "Make sure that

she knows that if she doesn't return I'll have them both picked up for conspiracy."

"How can I persuade her?"

"Promise her anything. But make sure that the militia will deal with the Jacobite as soon as she has left."

"And Ty Celyn?"

"That's up to you. I don't let my farms to idiots, and if I am obliged to get them both arrested it will be some time before I can take possession. By then I shall have found someone more suitable than you. But I don't want it that way. You'll need money." He threw several coins on to the table. "See to it man, for your own sake!"

Jencyn was in an ill humour when he returned to his cottage. He felt that he had been given an impossible task. His own powers of persuasion over Catrin he rated as nil, even with the direst threats.

Jenette was nursing the baby as she ladled his broth, and again Jencyn felt that twisted anger which always filled him when he looked at the lusty infant. On many occasions he wondered if he had in fact carried out God's will when he married Jenette. His marriage had not brought him that tranquillity which he had imagined came in the wake of wedded bliss. Sexually, he felt even more frustrated than when in single life he had wrestled with himself to subdue his carnal nature. Watching the girl now, attending to her baby, helped him to draw up a plan.

"You will come with me to Cardiff tomorrow, Jenette." The girl looked up startled. "How can I go so far?" she protested. "There is the baby to consider."

"You will bring him."

"But he is too young to travel."

"I'm not bothered about your precious baby. What is he anyway but the price of sin? I don't doubt the devil will take care of his own."

Jenette's mouth settled into a sullen line. Her heart contracted in hatred for the man who sat at the table in the place which should have been Dic's, who sipped the broth which she should have been cooking for Dic, who had taken on the protection of Dic's baby, but who seemed likely to become his tormentor.

"Why do you ask me to go with you?"

"Because you are more likely to persuade Mistress Thomas to return than I. Our future depends on this, Jenette. If she marries Mr. Evans, then we are the tenants of Ty Celyn." Jencyn stood, his lips narrowed, his eyes firm. Did not the Bible say that wives should be subject to their husbands? "You are coming with me, Jenette, and you will do as I say."

Catrin and Simon waved goodbye to John as the cart lurched along the rough track, jerking the cheeses from their appointed places, and causing them to slither around the flat wooden bottom of the waggon, while the round faced women shrieked with laughter as they tried to retrieve them. John and the horses diminished into the distance as the river widened and the banks flattened and spread into broad meadows spangled with king-cups and marguerites.

Simon whispered plans to Catrin as they jogged along the miles, although their companions had little English and would have found it difficult to inform on anything overheard.

"The ship will leave in two days' time," he told

the girl. "During that time we will stay in different places so that you will not be in danger through association with me."

Catrin began to protest but Simon was insistent.

"We must take the utmost care," he went on. "Soon we will be together always, but only if all goes well. Mr. Morris had given me several addresses. There are many supporters of the Jacobite cause in the town. You will have to find a certain George Lewis, a barber, who lives in Womanby Street," he added.

The afternoon was warm, the ride interminable, or so it seemed to Catrin, but eventually the hamlets grew closer together, the road hardened and became less rutted, and the squawk of seagulls overhead told them that they were approaching the coast. The grey walls and the moat of a castle sprang on their right, the ivy-covered ruins of a friary, sprawling at the foot of a fine house built from its stones, on their left. Before they reached the North Gate of the town, Simon requested the driver to stop. He jumped from the cart heaving the tin trunk on to his shoulder.

"I'll see you at the Quayside in two hours' time," he whispered to Catrin as he left. "Then we can exchange news."

The girl felt a momentary pang of alarm as he disappeared among the throng of people clustered around the gate, even though previously she had insisted that she would have no fear in finding George Lewis's house alone, and that Simon must on no account accompany her. The waggon lumbered into the town where a motley of noisy folk skilfully avoided the press of horse traffic and carts. Catrin's companions become even more talkative, waving and

201

gesticulating to imagined acquaintances in the crowd and jumping up and down with excitement, until the driver turned and growled at them sourly. He stopped the cart and looked pointedly at Catrin.

"My thanks to you," She jumped to the ground, the women heartily shouting good byes as the cart moved on its dusty way.

Catrin stood awhile, bewildered by the bustle, by the surge of people, by the buildings and the horses. A noisy group had congregated nearby and Catrin moved towards them to investigate the cause of the commotion. She shuddered as she heard them shouting abuse at some poor fellow confined in the stocks. Sickened she turned away from the scene and found herself in a street of fine, tall houses, so grand, so different from the cottages and farmhouses of the *Blaenau* that she found some difficulty in persuading herself that they were real and not a figment of her imagination. She stood still in the street and took in every detail of their low gable fronts with storey projecting over storey, the oak mullions, the lead casement windows. A passer-by told her that this was Duke Street and Catrin found it a fitting name.

She was still gazing in wonderment when the door of one of the houses opened and a broad-shouldered man with cynical grey eyes descended the steps to the street. Although there was something familiar about his stance, Catrin did not immediately recognise him. Then she gasped. It was Captain Willoughby.

For a moment he regarded her haughtily. Then a smile of recognition spread across his features. He bowed. "My dear, Mistress ... Mistress ...."

"Thomas."

"Of course." He looked to right and left for an escort. "But you are alone?"

"I am staying with an uncle." Initially dismayed, Catrin determined that she would bluff out the encounter. "I have no servants with me."

"Then your uncle should ensure that you do not venture out by yourself. I will accompany you back to his house."

"I cannot encroach on your time."

"I have no business that cannot wait. Where are you bound?"

Catrin bit her lip. She had no wish to tell Captain Willoughby where she was staying, yet any reluctance on her part to disclose her address could be construed as suspicious. She was further discomfited by having no idea where to find the street in which George Lewis lived. She looked at the Captain boldly.

"You may accompany me as far as Womanby Street," she suggested.

"It will be my pleasure. My regret is that the distance is so short."

Catrin hoped that the Captain would not notice that she moved only after he had indicated the right direction, or how she lagged a little behind his steps so that he did not see what a stranger she was to her surroundings.

"Have you been in Cardiff long?"

"A few days only." Catrin could not admit to having just arrived, alone and with no luggage. This would surely strike the Captain as suspicious.

"Then you must permit me to show you

something of the town."

"With my uncle's permission," Catrin hedged.

They had turned into Womanby Street, a narrow road, which from the call of gulls and the tangy smell of the sea, evidently led to the Quay.

Catrin anxiously scanned the houses. These were simpler dwellings than those in Duke St., and some had shops incorporated into the lower storey. With sinking spirits Catrin wondered how she would find out which one housed George Lewis. Some of the shops had trade signs hung over the doors and from these it was easy to decipher what business was carried on inside. One sign mystified Catrin. This was a pole painted in red and white. She had never seen anything like it before.

Captain Willoughby chuckled. "You will find life in Cardiff very different from that in your simple hill country. For instance you would never deduce that the sign you are staring at with such amazement designates the dwelling of one of our barber-surgeons. The red paint represents the blood he is so fond of letting."

The Captain so enjoyed showing off his superior knowledge that he failed to notice the relieved smile which spread across Catrin's face. So this was where George Lewis, barber, lived.

"Now that you have brought me to my uncle's street, I will not detain you any longer."

"On the contrary. I'll see you to your house."

Catrin bowed to the inevitable. She approached the barber's shop and knocked at the door.

"This is your uncle's house?" Captain

Willoughby's voice was surprised and held a faint trace of irritation.

The door was opened by a burly man of middle age who looked straight past Catrin to the Captain, his black brows beetling with anger. He stepped forward belligerently.

"Leave me alone. You can prove nothing."

Captain Willoughby smiled superciliously. "I have not called concerning your various appearances in Court. I have brought your niece back safely. You should see that she is not allowed to wander around alone. The streets are not safe as you very well know."

"It is not my Uncle's fault. You told me to be careful, didn't you Uncle?" Catrin pressed her fingers into the man's forearm as she spoke and her eyes pleaded with him for understanding.

George Lewis hesitated, then fathoming something of the girl's dilemma, he jerked his head towards the inside of the house.

"Your Aunt is in there. Go and explain to her where you have been." He threw a black look towards Captain Willoughby, and stepping back into the house slammed the door.

Catrin stood in the tiny kitchen where Mrs. Lewis was busy kneading dough.

"So, we have a niece, Elizabeth." George Lewis joined them and regarded Catrin with cautious amusement. "What have you done, my girl, to be hoodwinking the good Captain in this manner?"

"Not as much as you, I'll be bound," Elizabeth added shrilly. She turned to Catrin. "Wearing oak leaves he was, on June 10th., the Pretender's

Birthday."

"James IIIs' birthday," amended George. "Proud I am to be coming up in court for it."

"Fines, fines, nothing but fines. Anyone would think we had money to throw in the Taff. And he's been drinking the Pretender's health in public. 'God send our King well home from Lorraine' ", the woman mimicked, " 'and let the man have his mare again.' "

"Stop your snivelling, woman," George roared. "My opinions are as good as anyone's and speak up I will till my dying day for what I think is right."

"With never a care how his wife suffers." The woman sniffed and continued to pummel and tear at the sticky mess she was kneading.

"Perhaps I had better go elsewhere," Catrin began. "I don't want to get you into further trouble."

"First, tell us what you want from us," the woman told her sharply.

Briefly, Catrin explained the purpose of her visit, and as she heard the girl's story, Elizabeth's face softened. "Don't take any notice of my nagging," she said. "Of course you shall stay here. I agree with George," she added, "but it wouldn't do to let him have his own way all the time."

She showed Catrin upstairs to a small bedroom set under the eaves. "Very small it is," she said, "but it should serve you for a couple of nights. And now I'll find you something to eat, for you will be hungry after so long a time travelling."

Catrin was indeed grateful for the meal she provided, consuming with enjoyment the cold chicken and the vegetables fresh from the garden behind the shop. There was good white wine to swill it down and raisins and nuts which Mrs. Lewis said had been imported from France.

Soon it was time to think of meeting Simon at the Quay, and when he learned of her plans, George insisted on accompanying Catrin.

"As Captain Willoughby said, it is neither wise nor seemly for a young lady to venture out alone. Particularly this is true of the Quayside, where the sailors are rough and have little concern for the niceties of life."

The scene at the Quay filled Catrin with wonder. The river, deep now that it was coming up to high tide, was amazingly broad, although George assured her that as rivers went, the Taff was a stripling. In the distance a ship was approaching, a brigantine George said, its two masts tall against the sky and silhouetted like a dark etching against the rosy suffusion of the dying day.

"It's huge," Catrin breathed, her eyes wide with wonder as the vessel rode the tide gracefully towards harbour.

"Not as large as the ship which will take us to the New World."

"Simon!" Catrin turned sharply and found her husband close behind her. She wanted to throw herself into his arms; to hold him closely, with love and with relief that they were still safe, still together. Only with the utmost constraint did she curtsey conventionally, recognising in Simon's answering bow, the same suppressed ardour. She was grateful for George's discretion, for after a brief introduction he stood aside while the couple explored the Quayside together.

Catrin stepped daintily over the coiled ropes which lay in strategic places, avoided baskets tangy with fish, and smiled nervously into the faces of the fishermen and sailors, who leaned against the wall or squatted on drums, sucking at short clay pipes, their beards rough on skins dry and brown from salt and wind.

All the while Catrin and Simon exchanged news. Only a short while had passed since their parting, but already there was so much to tell. Catrin was surprised to learn that Simon knew of her encounter with Captain Willoughby.

"I followed you from a distance," he told her. "You had not imagined that I would leave you to fend for yourself with no one to come to your rescue if you were in trouble!"

The Captain gained no information from me," Catrin assured her husband, and jokingly told him of her adoption of George Lewis as "uncle".

The brigantine was drawing nearer and Catrin and Simon watched its progress on the clear water and then, as it docked at the Quay, listened to the buzz of activity, the calls and shouts as ropes were tightened and the creaking timbers came to a grinding halt.

Simon's arm tightened around Catrin's waist. "This is the vessel which will take us to France," he told her. "Tomorrow it discharges its cargo and takes on a load of skins and butter and wool. The following day we sail in her for La Rochelle."

Catrin held her breath. French sailors were chattering around her in a language which sounded like water over pebbles. A man climbed up the rigging with a speed and agility incredible to her. The thought of days spent at sea with dry land only a promise in the distance alarmed her, but also keyed her with excitement. Her fingers trembled as she held Simon's arm. Life was frightening but wonderful!

She felt a hand on her shoulder and turned her head in surprise to find George standing next to her, his eyes guarded, his mouth taut and grim.

"It grows chilly. Elizabeth will want you back." His words brooked no argument, held a warning note, and Catrin looking beyond him saw Captain Willoughby approach from the opposite direction. She sensed, rather than saw, Simon vanish into the throng around the newly docked vessel, and despite the throbbing of her pulse, by the time the Captain bowed in front of her, she had regained her composure.

"This scene will be new to you, Mistress Thomas." "Indeed it is, and very exciting too. Nevertheless, I must take my leave of you, sir. My aunt is expecting me back."

George nodded stiffly, and drew her away from the Quayside. His thick body was a bulwark of strength, challenging the sophisticated danger that lurked in Captain Willoughby's mocking eyes. As Catrin turned into Womanby St., she could almost feel his gaze following her and she wondered uneasily if he had in fact seen her with Simon. Perhaps he was even now piecing facts together, planning enquiries.

She trembled slightly with apprehension. If only they could sail that night! There was another day to live through. A day of tension and caution, of fearing and hoping, a day which, in Catrin's imagination, stretched on an on, interminably.

FOURTEEN

Yet, the next morning passed quickly for Catrin, so enthralled was she by the sights and sounds of her new surroundings, by the busy clatter of the nearby Quay, by the scream of sea birds as they swooped on tit-bits of food, by the iron strike of hooves on cobbles, by the trundle of waggons, by the hub-bub of country folk arriving at the West Gate with their products, for it was Market Day.

Elizabeth Lewis accompanied Catrin to the busy stalls in the town Centre, and for a while the girl was even able to forget the threat posed by Captain Willoughby as between the mounds of butter and cheese, the lengths of cloth, the leather ware and the products of potter and cooper, she heard cheap-jacks and peddlers plying their goods, and watched tumblers and jugglers who struggled to entertain the passers-by and draw a few pence from their pockets in consequence. Someone had brought a bear on a length of chain and a space was cleared in front of the Guild Hall where the poor creature, under provocation, moaned and twisted on his hind legs, his tortured movements evidently passing as a dance, for all the while, a pipe was playing.

The busy scenes around the Guild Hall, the Shambles and the Corn Stores, were distracting enough, held enough wonder and interest to ease

Catrin's impatience for the afternoon. George had told her at breakfastime, that he would then take her to visit Simon.

"He is lodging with a friend of mine at the Hayes," he informed Catrin. "We have advised him not to wander abroad during the day. He took a risk yesterday, but with luck, no harm has been done."

"You are taking a risk too, Mr. Lewis. How can we thank you?"

"By getting away safely. My reward will be to see you getting the better of Captain Willoughby and those like him. With fine talk and long pockets, they think themselves better than folk like us; folk who have worked hard and remained true to their convictions and their country. But they shall not have everything their own way. Not while George Lewis is around to harass them!"

Catrin smiled uncertainly, but while her host's motives were somewhat ambiguous, of his loyalty there could be no doubt. After a simple meal at mid-day, she set off in his company to find Simon's lodgings.

John Sweet's cottage at the Hayes was a simple affair, set in a garden where hens scratched at the dust and a sow lay drowsy in the sun despite the attentions of a bevy of suckling pigs. A small child kept watch at the gate and when he saw Mr. Lewis approach with Catrin, ran inside with a warning.

Their progress had been noted however by John Sweet, so that when Catrin entered the cottage she found herself in Simon's arms.

"I was ready to fly upstairs and merge into the

furniture had it been anyone more sinister," he told her. "But 'tis you, my dearest Kate."

He told her how before dawn, he had visited the Quay where the brigantine, *La Reine,* was now safely anchored, and had spoken to the master of the ship, who although a Frenchman was a sympathiser, and who also possessed the sort of spirit which needed the spice of adventure to survive.

"Our chest is already on board," he added. "The ship sails at noon tomorrow. We must be ready to join her just before she leaves."

Catrin clung to Simon, not caring that George Lewis and John Sweet were busy talking sedition in the ingle-nook, or that Mrs. Sweet was desperately trying to calm a crying baby. All that mattered was that Simon was with her, that she could feel his arms enclose her, that she could touch the rough stubble on his cheek, that she could draw strength from the calm and gentle blue eyes which bathed her with a loving glow.

"God will protect us, Catrin," he whispered. "God and His Blessed Mother." He felt, rather than saw, the slight shiver which ran through his wife's frame; he sensed the cloud of doubt which shadowed her. "Have faith, little Kate. We haven't come this far to be parted again. Remember your dream; remember Mary of Penrhys!"

Catrin nodded, saw again the burning statue of her dream and the rubies which changed to a shower of gold. The memory comforted her when George Lewis drew her from the cottage, reminding her that their presence there might draw the attention of the law-keepers of the town.

"The Constable and the Bailiffs take too much interest in my activities and in those of John Sweet," he explained and his fleshy lips curled with satisfaction. George Lewis took a delight in being a thorn in the flesh of officialdom. "Now we will return and you will not venture out again until high tide tomorrow morning. Nothing must go wrong at this stage."

As they left the house, Catrin noticed that the sky above the little town was peppered with scudding clouds which were massing together in black banks, threatening to dim the sun which fringed their curved edges with gold. A rising wind whipped Catrin's skirts around her ankles and brought problems to the stall holders who endeavoured to anchor their wares and improvise shelter from the growing severity of the blast.

The crowd jostled and pushed and George Lewis, his hand firmly grasping Catrin's elbow purposefully forged a path, his stocky body leaning heavily on the mass of people. Catrin followed breathlessly, bewildered by the throng around her, scarcely gaining more than an impression of the buyers and sellers, the sheep and the geese, the horses and dogs, the cacophony of sound which accompanied the transactions.

They had passed the Guildhall, and were nearing the turning which led to the Quay and to George's home, when Catrin stopped, her fingers tightening around her escort's arm.

"What is it, Catrin?" George Lewis turned around looking in alarm at the girl's face, now suddenly white and drawn.

"Nothing." She shook her head vehemently. "A passing fancy. I thought I saw ... My mind is playing games. Take no notice of me."

She smiled, trying to put her fears behind her as they walked towards Womanby Street. Anxiety was leading her to strange imaginings. How could Jencyn be in Cardiff? Yet for a fleeting second she had thought that he stood watching her, his sober suit deepening the intensity of his black eyes which momentarily held hers, challengingly, triumphantly. She shook away her fancies and went indoors to partake of the meal Mrs. Lewis had waiting for her.

Jencyn had wandered around the market for an hour, his fertile mind surprisingly unable to supply him with plans, ideas, solutions. He and Jenette had arrived at the West Gate of the town a little after noon, the girl fearful, the baby crying, the horses sweating, one of them lamed. Fortunately there was an inn, the Angel, close by and an ostler took charge of their mounts while a servant showed them to a room on the first floor and brought them food and ale. The crowds, the size of the town alarmed them, but Jencyn could not afford to be intimidated. He had a mission to accomplish. His whole future depended on its success.

"You will stay here," he ordered Jenette. "I will go into the town and make enquiries."

Standing outside in the shadow of the high walls of the Castle, he was at a loss. The country folk milled through the West Gate, parking their horses in a long sweaty row beneath the battlemented Tower. A steady stream of people moved towards the Market and Jencyn found himself drawn with them to the booths and stalls set up around the Shambles and for a while he forgot the purpose of his visit as he watched the bartering and argument as goods exchanged hands. He felt a strange exhilaration at the size of the town, the prosperity of many of the inhabitants, at the prices charged for produce he would have taken for granted. Two shillings and sixpence for a goose! He could have brought several such themselves, or even bought them from small farmers on the way, and then what a profit he would have made! For a moment the vision of a life that did not involve back-breaking work shone in front of Jencyn, but he recalled himself quickly to his task.

It was an impossible one. The few people he asked laughed in his face. "Have we seen a strange young woman? You ask us this on Market Day? Go home and say your prayers, sober-sides!"

Jencyn was despairing, but his eyes were sharp and when he caught a glimpse of a dark haired girl with a face as bewildered as his own, being pulled through the crowds by a burly, aggressive looking man, he quickly pushed his way nearer. It was Catrin surely and for a moment, to his annoyance, his eyes met hers and saw there fleeting recognition. Then he melted into the crowd like a mirage, following the couple distantly and unobserved. He watched as they turned into Womanby Street and took careful note of the building they entered. It would be easy to find again. The long barber's pole outside provided brilliant identification.

Jencyn was jubilant when he returned to the Inn. "I have found her," he told Jenette. "Now it is up to you. You will go there and talk her into returning."

"That is impossible. What woman in her right

senses would want Griffith Evans served up for breakfast?"

"No one would choose to live in poverty when a comfortable life with ease and luxury was the alternative." Jencyn's cheek twitched as he remembered his own hungry past. His eyes glinted as he thought despairingly towards his own future. "If she is so stupid, then you must threaten her. You remember all I told you on the way?"

Jenette nodded dully.

"Then we have her. Somewhere in this town we will find someone in charge of the militia. If you do not succeed, I will start enquiries immediately."

Catrin had eaten and was scattering corn to the hens at the back of the barber's shop when George came from the house and looked at her uneasily.

"There is a girl asking for you," he told her. "A girl with a baby. I cannot deny that you are here for Captain Willoughby knows of your presence. Will you see her?"

"Jenette. It can only be Jenette."

Catrin's heart was beating wildly as she re-entered the house and ran into the small parlour where the other girl stood tearfully, the baby at her breast.

"Mistress Thomas, please forgive me, but Jencyn ... he made me come, for he said that you would listen to me. But I know that you will not, for how can you ..? how could anyone ...?

"Calm yourself, Jenette. Do I understand that Jencyn knows where I am and has sent you to bring me back to Ty Celyn?"

Jenette nodded and sniffed as the tears rolled

down her cheeks. "And he threatens . . . all sorts of things . . . the militia ... he says you are mixed up with the Jacobites and could get hung or transported."

Fear crawled along Catrin's spine and her muscles tightened apprehensively, but her lips set in a firm line and her eyes glinted dangerously.

"You can tell Jencyn that I shall never return of my own free will. And if he wants to threaten ... let him do what he will. I will fight back."

"I'll tell him." Jenette's eyes gleamed admiringly as she left. "Good fortune, Mistress Thomas. I wish you well."

Alone in the small room, Catrin found herself shaking. Only a few hours stood between happiness and disaster. How she wished that she and Simon were even now on *La Reine* and sailing away from fear and suspicion and threat. She said as much when she explained Jenette's visit to George.

"You would hardly wish to be at sea tonight," he commented and Catrin became aware of the rising wind which now battered the eaves of the house, throwing rain like fistfuls of gravel at the mullioned windows.

"I'll go across to John Sweet's house and warn your husband," George went on. "It's still best for you to lie low and get on board at the last possible moment. John Sweet and I will be out this evening with our eyes skinned and our ears well trimmed for what we can see and hear."

Jencyn too was abroad in the driving rain which had put an early close to the market, and was hampering the efforts of the stall holders to pack away their goods. He had not been surprised when Jenette brought back her message, a triumphant note strengthening her voice.

"Not for anything will she go back, Jencyn. Do your worst, she says. She will fight to the end."

"And so will I. No sympathy have I for the woman now. If she chooses to consort with Jacobites and Papists she will pay the price. You will stay here, Jenette. I have work to do."

Drawing his cloak around his shoulders and placing his wide-brimmed hat firmly on his head, Jencyn pushed his way through the driving storm. The Guildhall was his first objective where the Clerks of the Market were busy collecting their tolls. They had little time for Jencyn who, they considered, cut a comic figure in his shabby country clothes, with his insistence that he had news of treason and intrigue.

"To the Lord Lieutenant you should be going, Longshanks," they told him with raucous laughter. "Try the Shire Hall. They have more time there for nonsense."

So Jencyn turned his face towards the Castle, but his reception there meant more indignity. He was interviewed by a stout gentleman in a gaudy embroidered suit and a full-bottomed wig who took snuff incessantly, dribbling it down his swollen waistcoat. He did not speak to Jencyn directly but addressed his remarks through an obsequious clerk.

"Tell the man that we are constantly pestered by idiots in search of reward or revenge. If he has something of import for the militia he should approach Captain Willoughby."

"Captain Willoughby?"

Jencyn felt sudden hope spring inside him. If he could get hold of him, Captain Willoughby would surely listen. He would not have forgotten Catrin Thomas easily.

"He lives in Duke Street," the clerk told him. "Call at his house."

The door was opened by a footman in livery who looked down on Jencyn with disdain.

"The Captain is not in," he said. "But I doubt if he would see you."

"I have important information," Jencyn protested. "A matter of treason."

"In that case, come back later."

The door was firmly closed in Jencyn's face, leaving him in a sweat of frustration. He pushed himself back into the lashing rain, the fierce drops washing some of his irritation away as he strode along the street. There was little purpose in his steps, but presently he found himself at the Quayside where the water lapped angrily at the stone wall and the wind cut through the rigging on the tall masts of *La Reine,* whistling and moaning as it battered the furled sails and drove cascades of rain on to the glistening deck and hull.

Jencyn looked at the vessel reflectively and a supposition which rapidly hardened into certainty sprang to his mind. A dark visage sailor stood next to him, sheltering in the arch of a doorway.

"Do you speak English?"

"A leetle."

"When do you sail?"

"Tomorrow. At the noon tide."

"Do you have passengers?"

The man's face became closed, enigmatic; he could not or would not understand.

"Passengers," repeated Jencyn. "A man and a woman. Are they sailing with you?" He drew a silver coin from his pocket and significantly showed it to the sailor.

The man's eyes widened and after a slight hesitation he nodded. *"Oui.* Mr. and Mrs. Johnson. They join us before we sail."

He quickly pocketed the coin and vanished into a nearby tavern. Jencyn stood for a few moments gazing at the rain-washed vessel, triumph and relief written on his features. Now he really had some concrete news for the Captain when he succeeded in finding him. He turned quickly and made his way back to the Angel. Jenette's presence was causing him some misgivings. He realised now that he had been foolish to bring her. He should have known that Catrin Thomas was so stubborn that she made nonsense out of reason, and Jenette had of late been throwing him glances which unnerved him. A man should not have cause to mistrust his wife, yet nevertheless he wished to get back to the hotel room to see that she was safely waiting there.

He pushed open the door of the Angel, glad of the shelter it afforded from the elements, but before he put a foot on the stairs, a loud voice raised in banter drew him into the inn parlour.

Captain Willoughby was sprawled at one of the tables, a jug of wine in front of him, a long pipe in his hand. He looked insolently at Jencyn as the man tried to explain his mission.

"I must speak to you," he insisted, "and privately. It concerns treason ... and Catrin Thomas."

Captain Willoughby's eyebrows lifted and a sparkle appeared in his eyes.

"Come upstairs with me," urged Jencyn. "I know a place where we can talk."

He led the way up the stairs and to a closet used by the still-room maids when they sorted laundry. He had noticed the room on his arrival as it was next to the chamber he and Jenette occupied.

"I'll fetch a light." The June evening was dark with storm and the room ill-lit by one small window.

In the bed-chamber Jenette sat on the edge of the bed, nursing Huw. She looked up sharply as Jencyn entered and took away her candle, leaving her to the greyness of the deepening dusk. She felt defeated, wrapped in a cocoon of helplessness, too afraid to contemplate the years ahead. She clutched the small child to her desperately, wanting so much for him, yet so afraid that his life would be one of rejection and hardship.

For a moment the voices penetrating the wall meant nothing to her. Then she heard the name *Catrin Thomas* mentioned and realised that Jencyn was speaking urgently to someone who could only be Captain Willoughby. The voices were clear and in amazement Jenette put her hand to the wall which divided the two rooms. Some plaster crumbled over her fingers and she realised that the rooms were really one, but had been divided by a thin partition.

She listened as Jencyn explained his suspicions, his certainty, that the missing couple were going to escape the country on the following day.

"I would take no notice of your imaginings if I had not seen the couple together on the Quay yester evening. You say that they are to travel as Mr. and Mrs. Johnson?" Captain Willoughby paused while Jencyn affirmed this fact and Jenette listened attentively and prayed that the baby would not cry. "I shall have men there tomorrow as the ship sails. It will be as well for you, my man, for you to be right."

Jenette heard footsteps descend the stairs and she was sitting again on the bed when Jencyn brought back the candle which sent shadows flickering around the room.

"I'm going out for a while." Jencyn felt overwrought. He could not bear to confine himself to the small Inn bedroom and the dubious pleasure of Jenette's company. There was a touch of irony in his voice as he added, "You will be glad to know that things are going our way at last."

For a while Jenette sat in silence nursing her baby. Her mind raced in a mad turmoil. Her own situation oppressed her. She felt trapped, and like a caged bird she wanted to fling herself at the walls of her prison, seeking freedom and the opportunity to give her son the good things of life. Now it seemed an even worse fate awaited Catrin Thomas than had been meted out to her. She wanted to help her former Mistress but beyond calling at her lodging with a warning there seemed little that she could do. Yet there must be some way out of the difficulty if only she thought hard enough. Jenette put her mind to the problem and from the desperation born of her circumstances, she found the answer.

FIFTEEN

Jenette arrived at the barber's shop just as George Lewis returned home. Catrin was about to retire to bed and she stared in alarm as George led the other girl, wild eyed and dishevelled from the wind, into the house. The baby, stirring beneath the protective shawl which Jenette wore across her shoulders, began to cry restlessly as his mother strove to regain her breath.

"Danger there is," she gasped, and stretching out her hand she clutched at Catrin's sleeve. "Jencyn has told Captain Willoughby everything. The militia will be waiting at the ship when you board."

Catrin felt faint with shock, and her eyes drenched with bleak dismay, turned to George for support. His brow was black and his lips formed a curse. The air in the small room suddenly became stifling, heavy with threat.

"Can we board immediately? Hide somewhere on the vessel?" Catrin's appeal was urgent, held a trace of desperation. "We cannot lose everything now!"

"The militia will be expecting passengers," George replied. "If no one turns up, the ship will be upended in the search to find them."

"I have a solution." Jenette's lips trembled with the temerity of her plan, and the glance she threw at Catrin was desperate with pleading. "Can you ... will you take me to the New World? I will serve you and

Mr. Johnson faithfully, and so will Huw when he is older. He will be strong. See ... She pulled the baby's arm from the shawl. "His hands are broad. He will be tall like Dic, and a hard worker too."

"How can this help us get away? You will just be putting yourself in danger too. And what of Jencyn, your husband?"

"I have no husband. I had no choice when I made those vows." Jenette's lips became a thin line and her eyes flashed dangerously. "Jencyn will raise my son as a slave. Mistress, if you and Mr Johnson hide in the ship tonight, I will go on board tomorrow. I will tell Captain Willoughby that I am Mrs. Johnson, and that my husband has decided to follow on a later ship. Lucky it is that he does not know that I am Jencyn's wife."

Catrin looked hesitantly at George Lewis. "It might work," he said thoughtfully. "It could be your only chance. But do you want this young woman at your side?"

"I needn't stay with you always," Jenette broke in. "When we get to the New World, I can find another position."

"Nonsense!" Catrin touched the girl's hand. "We will need help and I have enough money for the passage and our immediate needs. How will you get away from Jencyn tomorrow?"

"Clever you are with herbs, Mistress Thomas. Can you not give me something to make Jencyn sleep for some hours?"

"I can help." Elizabeth Lewis, who had been listening to the conversation unlocked a wooden cabinet which stood in the corner of the room and brought out a small phial. She handed it to Jenette. "This is syrup of poppy seed," she said. "It was made up for me recently when I suffered raging toothache and could not sleep. Give your husband half an ounce and he will sleep deeply for four or five hours."

Jenette pocketed the container with trembling fingers. "I will see that he has the potion with buttermilk or warm ale when it nears noon," she replied. "I must go back now or I shall be missed. Mistress Thomas ... thank you."

She disappeared into the night and the storm, and George pulled on his greatcoat again and pushed his hat well down over his ears.

"Going now I am to warn that husband of yours," he told Catrin. "We will see the master of the ship and fix everything up. Be ready to leave when I return." He paused as the wind drove an empty barrel noisily over the cobblestones outside and a flurry of rain spat at the window. George's face grew grim. "You can take refuge on the ship tonight," he commented darkly, "but that doesn't mean that you will be sailing tomorrow. No ship will leave harbour in this storm!"

He left and as the door opened a gust of wind shook the curtains and whistled boldly around the women's ankles. Elizabeth Lewis notices Catrin's stricken face and hastened to comfort her.

"Only a summer storm this is," she said reassuringly. "If it was winter the wind and the rain might stay for days, but at this time of the year ... believe me, my dear, it will pass."

Catrin wished she could believe her, but the tempestuous sound of the driving rain outside, beating a relentless tattoo on door and wall, washed away any reassurance she might have gained. When George returned and Elizabeth bade her God-speed, she pulled her cloak around her tightly and felt the knot of fear inside her grow and harden. Paradoxically, she drew strength from it, alarm tensing her muscles, powering her to follow George's progress in the teeth of the gale. Simon was waiting at the Quay, and Catrin clung to him, ignoring the rain which soaked through their clothes and ran in rivulets down their cheeks. George clasped their hands before he hastened away, his parting words lost in the fury of the storm, and then Simon helped Catrin along an unsteady gangway and on to the water lashed deck of *La Reine.* Opening a hatchway, he guided her along a narrow corridor and then into a cabin where a burly black bearded man in a red shirt sat at a table, his large fist clutching a brandy bottle, so saving it from lurching to the floor as the ship listed to the side. He told his visitors to take off their drenched outer clothing and then poured them spirits to chase away the effects of the elements.

"So ... leetle Mees!" He threw a bold but warm glance at Catrin. "You are expecting to sail tomorrow? Then say your prayers!"

"That, we will do." Simon's strong fingers wound around Catrin's and a flood of comfort swept through her, melting tension and fear. She and Simon were together, would be together ... had to be together for always!

"Stay in my cabin until daybreak," the ship's master went on. "Then you must find a hiding place. I carry a cargo of good skins and cloth. They will give you cover. I, Monsieur Duval, will hide you myself."

Catrin was glad of the brandy. It fired the back of her throat and sent warm blood coursing through the veins which had hitherto been chill with apprehension. She refused the cold chicken which Monsieur Duval pressed on her and Simon, too, scarcely did it justice. They were aware through the night of the floor shifting uncertainly under their feet, of the ship's timber, creaking and groaning under the onslaught of the wind, of the candle on the table sporadically spitting and guttering in the draught. The hours of darkness were interminable, but just before the first pale rays of dawn lit the small window of the cabin, Catrin realised with a burst of hope that the squally rain no longer hammered on the deck, and the wind, fury spent, had died away to a mere whisper.

Duval, sprawled in sleep across the table, roused himself and staggered to the window. He yawned and blinked at the sky, pale gold in the watery sun's promised path.

"Your prayers-they are answered. The storm, eet is finished. We will sail today! And now we will make you safe from the soldiers. At once, so that no one else on the ship will know. Only I, Monsieur Duval, will have the secret!"

Catrin and Simon followed him from the cabin and down into the hold of the vessel. On top of bales of woollen cloth and flannel were sheepskins and hides, piled high, seemingly in abandon.

"Now, my friends, you must crouch between these bales and I will cover you with the skins." His arm muscles bulging, Monsieur Duval lifted armfuls of hides so that Catrin and Simon could crawl over the woollen cloth until they found crevices where they were able to huddle.

"Bonne chance! I will enjoy the encounter with your Captain Willoughby."

The hides fell over the bales of cloth with a thud and Catrin stretched out her hands and her fingers wound around Simon's. It had been dark in the hold before, but now, beneath a layer of leather and sheepskin, cocooned between the large bales of sombre cloth, Catrin felt the blackness to be almost tangible. The air, warm with summer, was tangy with the smell of newly tanned hides, and after a while the closeness became almost unbearable.

"We must have patience," whispered Simon. "Have faith, little Kate. Soon now we will be out on the sea, heading for safety and our life together."

The serenity of his tones, his conviction that all would be well, his unshakeable belief that they would be protected from ill helped towards mitigating the sick dread which tortured Catrin's mind with frenzied imaginings. But there had been little opportunity to rest in the uncomfortable cabin during the night, and gradually the darkness, the warmth, the timelessness of her muffled existence made Catrin drowsy, and mercifully, she slept.

Jenette too, had scarcely slept during that night. The plan she had concocted had seemed simple enough to begin with, but now all kinds of difficulties sprang into her mind. Supposing Jencyn went out early, leaving her at the Inn? How could she be sure that he would drink the potion when she had prepared it? Would Captain Willoughby believe her story when she arrived at the ship? She was aware too that Jencyn was suffering from one of his sleepless nights. He tossed and turned restlessly, but Jenette feigned sleep, lying immobile with closed eyes, avoiding contact or conversation.

A breakfast of oatcakes and butter-milk was served early in their room. Jenette glanced at her husband nervously. "If you are going out this morning, will you take me with you?" she asked. "An adventure it is for me to come to Cardiff. Many questions will I be asked when we return to Ty Celyn."

Jencyn grunted. It suited him to keep Jenette close by his side. She did not know his plans, and even if she did, Jencyn would not have credited that a wife could betray him. Nevertheless, he did not want to risk the possibility of her visiting Catrin Thomas again. "Very well, Jenette. An appointment have I made to be at the Quayside at noon, but before that we will wander around the town."

So for a couple of hours the couple stayed close, each guarding the other, pretending an interest they were both too tense to feel at the sights offered by the small town, by the Castle, the ancient Gates, the Guild Hall, the churches, St. John's and St. Mary's, the latter battered by the winter floods, roofless and deserted.

Jenette nervously watched the sun climb the sky and at length judged it sufficiently high for her to feign exhaustion.

"I must return to the Inn," she begged Jencyn. "Although it is not yet time for a meal, I need refreshment. Warm ale I would like, and you too, will find need for the same, I am sure."

To her dismay Jencyn bought only one mug of ale. He brought it to their room, an expression of

231

disapproval on his face.

"You must learn not to expect drinks between meals," he told her. "Ale at this Inn costs several pence, so I decided to forego mine."

He sat at the small table and emptying his pockets, began to count the coins he carried. Jenette's heart raced in desperation as she watched. Then turning her back on Jencyn, she drew the phial from her pocket and emptied it into the mug which was still three-quarters full.

"Jencyn!" she wailed, and putting down the mug she contorted her face and clasped her hands over her belly. "Sorry I am, but I can drink no more. Such sickness has suddenly come over me!"

Jencyn looked up in annoyance and fastened his gaze on the abandoned mug.

"Why don't you finish it, Jencyn?" Jenette suggested. "A pity it would be to waste all that money."

The man nodded and with a sour look on his face lifted the mug and drank deeply. He had, in fact, been very thirsty.

"A good ale," he commented, "but with a trace of bitterness."

He returned to his calculations while Jenette looked on anxiously. It took about five minutes for Jencyn's eyes to become heavy, for the coins to slip through his fingers, for his head to rest on the table in deep slumber.

Jenette hastily collected the few possessions she had brought with her, and winding one corner of her big shawl around the baby, she flung the rest over her shoulder drawing the end around her waist. So, with her baby tightly snug against her breast she hastened from the Inn and along the street which led to the Quay.

In the hold, Catrin had been alerted to wakefulness by the sound of feet tramping over the deck above.

"What is happening?" She spoke in an urgent whisper to Simon who pressed her hand reassuringly.

"I am glad you slept," he told her. "That was merciful for you. There has been much activity for a while, but now I think the soldiers are coming on board. Do not speak at present, Catrin, or we may be discovered."

Catrin felt the blackness around her to be almost tangible, pressing on her suffocatingly, and now every slight movement she made, each tiny rustle of her gown, even the minimal vibration of her breath, seemed magnified, intensified, so that if any pursuers drew near, she felt sure that they must be drawn to the hiding place.

Voices were frighteningly close. Catrin distinguished the tones of Monsieur Duval and then a voice which could only be Captain Willoughby's became audible.

"I assure you, Monsieur, that if I believed my suspects to be hiding on your ship, I would have every item of cargo removed on to the Quay."

"And I can assure you, *Capitaine,* that no wrongdoers hide on my ship."

Catrin became aware that the Captain and Monsieur Duval were not alone. Some of the bales were being pushed around and the hides and skins disturbed.

"I can also assure you, *Capitaine,* that if any damage is done to my ship or cargo, it will be a case for the highest authorities. Why do you not wait for my passengers to arrive before you search further?"

"Very well. But if they do not arrive, your ship will be delayed."

Catrin felt relief sweep over her as the footsteps and voices retreated. Immediately, the danger was removed, but Jenette still had to board the ship; still had to confront the soldiers who would meet her as she arrived.

Captain Willoughby strode on to the deck ahead of the the ship's master, his cold eyes hard with irritation. He glanced at the sky where the sun had almost reached its zenith and then surveyed the swollen river. The tide was about to ebb and so enable *La Reine* to coast down to the Bristol Channel, but the Captain knew that if no passengers arrived he would be obliged to delay the sailing and institute a thorough search of the vessel. The situation aggravated him as he had felt doubtful of Jencyn's story from the beginning. The man himself he regarded with contempt; his tale most likely the wanderings of an illiterate mind. Yet he knew that Catrin Thomas was in Cardiff, and also that she was staying with a known Jacobite sympathiser. He had also seen her at the Quayside talking earnestly to a tall young man who might well be his quarry. The circumstances were too suspicious to be ignored, and so Captain Willoughby stood on deck, arrogantly surveying the growing crowd.

The departure of a vessel always attracted

sightseers, but today their numbers were swollen by the curiosity engendered by the presence of militia men. If an arrest or capture was made, no one wished to miss the event!

Their very presence annoyed the Captain. His work was not to provide entertainment for dolts! He found his anger rising. He had arranged to meet a crony for gaming at mid-day and he determined that if he was obliged to miss his appointment, by God he would make a good job of searching this ship, damage or no damage.

"Monsieur, where are these passengers?" He turned impatiently to the Frenchman.

"They will arrive soon. Patience, *Capitaine* ..." But Monsieur Duval's eyes were also anxiously scanning the crowd. This girl ... why did she not arrive?

A commotion on the Quayside drew the attention of the two men and they watched as a young woman carrying a shawled infant pushed her way through the melee and argued with the militia men on the wharf. She boarded the ship and stood before them, boldly, and with a trace of defiance.

"I am Mrs. Johnson, passenger on this ship."

"You are Mrs. Johnson?"

Captain Willoughby looked at Jenette with close, suspicious eyes. The girl was glad when the ship's master turned to her with an effusive greeting.

"Welcome, welcome, Meesis Johnson. And now," he turned triumphantly to the Captain, "now, may we sail?"

"With one passenger only? I was expecting two. Give me a good reason why I should not search your ship."

"I can give you a good reason." Jenette's voice rang clear and determined and she pulled the shawl away from her baby's head. "Here is the other passenger. This is *Mister* Johnson."

She held Captain Willoughby's eyes challengingly. When the black cloud of doubt cleared from his face he laughed derisively. "I should have known better than to listen to that fool of a Welsh pig. You can go Monsieur, and the rest of your rag-taggle mob with you." He strode on to the Quay and gave orders to the sergeant who barked at the militia, lining them in rough order, in competition with the milling crowds.

Monsieur Duval lost no time in issuing his orders too, and soon the deck was alive with activity as hawsers were loosened and the vessel edged away from the Quayside and began its slow drift to the Channel.

Jenette swayed uncertainly until a crew member led her to a cabin. There she sat and watched, numbly, through the window, as the river broadened and the ship established an ever lengthening barrier of water between her and Jencyn.

Still in the gloom of their hiding place, Catrin and Simon felt the ship roll as the wharf was left behind. The gentle sway, to which they had become accustomed during the dark hours of their concealment, intensified as the timbers creaked in tune with the movement of the vessel.

"We have left shore, Catrin. Soon we will be safe."

The next half-hour seemed interminable as they both controlled their desire to rush from their hiding place. When he felt that sufficient time had elapsed to put an effective distance between them and their pursuers, Simon pushed at the heavy hides which rested on top of the bales surrounding them. Catrin rose from her cramped position to help him heave them to one side.

"Take my hand." Simon freed himself from the confines of his refuge, and leaping on top of the bales, pulled Catrin up beside him. They edged themselves through the cargo until they were able to reach a corridor which led them to the upper regions of the ship. The light on deck was blinding after their long concealment in the hold, the breeze refreshingly pure.

"Come Catrin, we are clear of the river."

The girl felt an arm encircle her waist as Simon drew her to the prow of the vessel. She stood, leaning against the firmness of his body, his supporting arms steadying her against the rocking motion which she felt beneath her feet. Her cheeks were whipped by the wind and her hair tossed high as the unfurled square sails on the tall mast behind her, billowed in a wide arc.

Sea birds dipped and glided overhead, the water below them, iridescent in the sunlight, was etched with moving patterns of foam.

They were scudding past cliffs and a panorama of green hills beyond, at what seemed to Catrin an incredible rate. Those hills had been her home,that land had been bequeathed her by her fathers, and now all was growing distant and hazy beneath the afternoon sun.

Simon tilted her face towards him and his perceptive gaze understood the wave of *hiraeth,* of homesickness, which he read there.

"Look forward, little Kate," he urged. "So much lies ahead."

Catrin, her skin touched with salt-spray, turned to watch the sun throw fire on to the glittering water and gather up reflections until the Western sea and sky was transformed by a brilliant pattern of crimson and gold.

Catrin was reminded of the necklet of rubies. "We are sailing into a jewel," she whispered in wonder and in awe. "Our happiness lies within it."

POSTSCRIPT

Much has been written about the Rhondda Valley after the advent of the Industrial Revolution, when the iron works and coal pits desecrated the land. The action of this novel takes place before those days and before the Religious Revival which transformed the thinking of the Welsh people.

The curate I have mentioned in the novel is fictional and so I thought it best to refer to the parish as Llanfodwg. The area described was originally known as Ystradyfodwg and comprised a parallelogram of territory, approximately sixteen miles long by four miles wide and traversed by the Rhondda Fawr River. It stretched from present day Cymmer in the south, to Rhigos in the north.

The Shrine and Holy Well at Penrhys was a famous place of pilgrimage in the Middle Ages and until the Reformation. The oak statue of Our Lady was then carted off to London where it was burnt publicly together with the statue from Walsingham. The jewels with which it had been adorned over the years were confiscated for the Royal coffers.

George Lewis and John Sweet, minor characters in the concluding chapters, appear in local records as Jacobite sympathisers and were constantly fined for harassing the authorities. Mr. and Mrs. Morris of Llantarn are based on a couple called Matthews who lived at Llancaiach near Merthyr Tydfil. When her husband died in 1726 an action was brought against Anne Matthews for recovery of her property, as her brother-in-law claimed that she was unable, as a

Catholic, to inherit. Father Davies was a native of Montgomery and worked for 54 years in the area, dying at Llanarth, Gwent in 1761 aged 84.

ND - #0477 - 270225 - C0 - 203/127/20 - PB - 9781909129573 - Matt Lamination